BLOCK LEGEND PAPER
BY THE TON I

KEVIN GREEN

authorHOUSE

AuthorHouse™
1663 Liberty Drive
Bloomington, IN 47403
www.authorhouse.com
Phone: 833-262-8899

Published by AuthorHouse 11/04/2020

ISBN: 978-1-6655-0697-7 (sc)
ISBN: 978-1-6655-0696-0 (e)

Print information available on the last page.

Any people depicted in stock imagery provided by Getty Images are models, and such images are being used for illustrative purposes only.
Certain stock imagery © Getty Images.

This book is printed on acid-free paper.

WILL MY LUCK EVER CHANGE

I often wonder if my luck will ever change, hoping I don't get left out, stuck in the rain, staring off into space letting my mind drift again, thinking about life, and the things I go through, had a full box but its never enough to blow through, keeping my mind lifted, because its nothing to hold on to. So I hold on to the pain because sometimes that's all you have to hold on to, a box is never enough to blow through. I wonder if my luck will ever change, or will I get left out and stuck in the rain with the pain. So much pain staring off into space again, wondering if the sun will ever come out again, inhaling weed smoke again to ease my mind, loosing track of time searching to find peace of mind. Staring off into space, running out of time, I always feel like I'm running out of space, lost my motivation, maybe I just need a change of pace, forever fighting time, and losing the race, wondering if I should pick it up or keep my pace, wondering if my luck will ever change or will I loose the race, searching for another blunt to take to the face, stuck in the rain as I stare into space, where do I go from here, were will this road take me, holding on to life knowing that life might break me in two because of the things I do, sometimes I wish I could just start over and begin a new; what do I do, where do I go from here, where will this road take me, wondering when did my life start to hate me, hoping the blues shake me and ease my pain, stuck in the rain, inhaling weed smoke again, going through so much pain, driving down an empty highway dragging so much pain, how can I win driving on a road that leads to nowhere, stop smoking I don't dare. I just love the smell of weed in the air, driving on an empty highway just trying to find my way, wondering how did so many black clouds come my way, blowing O's at the rearview, hoping the sun comes out today, hoping the rain stops today, hoping the black clouds stop coming my way, hoping somehow, someway I'll find my way driving alone on this empty highway, watching the smoke bounce my way wiping the rain away, hoping the smoke takes the pain away, a lone driving on this deserted highway. Loosing track of time, doing what I gotta do to ease my mind, out here searching to find peace and peace of mind, when will my luck change, and wash away the pain sometimes I get tried of the rain, hoping to push the clouds away so the sun can shine again, as I put the blunt to my lips and another puff again searching for another blunt again, driving on a empty highway trying to find a way to win, hoping the sun comes out again, so I can live life again, listening to the wind hollowing, as the smoke fills the air, when will my luck change, driving on this empty highway that leads to nowhere, just trying to find my way, wondering when will my luck change and life start to go my way, driving on this empty highway, hoping the rains stops, and life starts to go my way, blowing O's watching the smoke float my way, just another dollar, another day hoping I don't get lost and my way, out here trying to find myself on this deserted highway, waiting for the day when life starts to go my way, I wonder if my luck will ever change, or will I forever be stuck in the rain, dealing with so much pain, dame there goes these black clouds again, hoping for the day when the sun comes out to shine again.

SO LONG LIFE

[Ain't no time for talking speaking words unsaid no turning back now, prepared to die until its off with my head, out here with a price on my head, they said I'm better off dead, prepared to die hoping they die instead.]

So, so long life, prepared for death knowing everyday standing could be my last one left, I seem to be running out of real niggas, I seem to be the last one left, so, so long life with just a roll of the dice, if my life is up then I'm prepared to pay the price, so put the dice in my hands and let me roll the dice, too hot to handle until I'm as cold ice. I keep the dice in my hands ready to roll the dice prepared to pay the price for life, prepared for death. So, so long life, here today gone tomorrow with just one roll of the dice so, so long life. Why does it seem like real die first and fake niggas die last, here today gone tomorrow with just one shot from the shotgun blast, these fake niggas can't last, hoping I ain't the last to blast, shoot first and ask questions last, hit em up, hit em high and then hit the gas, ready to hit em all when I pass, hoping I don't pass, but that's the price you pay, life is hard and around here niggas die everyday, so, so long life, I'm ready too pay, shoot em up bang bang, that's the price you pay, you stay where you lay, ain't no coming back from that, now it ain't no way in hell that nigga can bounce back, no time to act, just react, paying the price you pay, it's cold round here niggas die everyday. So, so long life here today gone tomorrow with one roll of the dice, I'm prepared for death ready to pay the price, pistal grip griped, now so long life. How can I win when I see death around every block I bend, knowing hard niggas die too. Sometimes life makes other niggas pay the price for you. If you ride with me, you gotta be prepared to die with me, never knowing when life may give up on you, ready to give it to em close range living life insane, here today gone tomorrow with just one shot to the brain no time to watch the rain, life is hard round here where everyday niggas shoot em up bang bang, every day is the same thang if them niggas were in my position they'd probably be doing the same thang, no talk for talking, just let yo nuts hang, dying around here seems to be an everyday thing. Somebody make that fat bitch sing, and tell life goodbye filling you up until I can't see that twinkle in your eye, so goodbye and so long life, here today gone tomorrow with just one roll of the dice, just another day surrounded by niggas ready to take my life, so put the dice in yo hands, nigga, and roll the dice and say hello to death nigga and so long life, its time to pay the price. I'm still standing but that niggas as cold as ice, just another day another doller another roll of the dice, I'm prepared to pay the price. So, so long life, when you live the hard life death is the price of life so so long life, kiss death in the face and say so long life.

NIGGA PLEASE

Nigga please, you can open up yo mouthpiece and suck on these. I pitty the fool trying to test these, nigga please I make chesse. I know you know better then to fuck with a nigga with nuts as swole as these, you might as well open up yo mouthpiece, and suck on these I know you know better then to fuck with Gee's like these nigga please.

Blow yo lights out like a candle got a 45 special that I love to handle put a hole in ya and make ya body desenagrate for these niggas that love to hate, the next bullet won't wait, so don't hate and don't test the techniq, I perfect the techniq to make yo head leak. I can't stop pulling the trigger until yo body goes weak, so go leak with yo head on ice I heard death is paradise so so long life. Though a nigga knew better then to fuck with Gee's like these you might as well open up yo mouthpiece and suck on these, got no time for fleas, you get tic's off yo with bullets like these nigga please. Don't fuck with Gee's like these, save the haters for later now it's time to make chesse, just look em in the face and tell them to suck on these.

Nigga please, you can open up yo mouthpiece and suck on these, I pitty the fool trying to test these. Nigga please I make chesse. I know you know better then to fuck with a nigga with nuts as swole as these. You might as well open up yo mouthpiece, and suck on these. I know you know better then to fuck with Gee's like these, Nigga please.

Nigga have laying down with his head on ice, but that's life, ain't no time for fronting when its the end of life, you reap what you soe with just a roll of the dice, sometimes death is the price, look death in the eye and say so long life, had to put a end to a nigga because I like to live my life, when you cross the game you have to ante up and pay the price, my 45 is my wife ain't nothing closer to me, put a nigga away, with you around death is closer to me, if you look in the niggas eye all you see is hate pointed at me just me and my 45 special ready to ride with me. Nigga please don't test me, introduce you to death personally for trying to test me, put you in the dirt by myself if they'd let me, wet a nigga just for trying to wet me. I tried to forget a nigga but my 45 won't let me.

- Nigga please, you can open up yo mouthpiece and suck on these. I pitty the fool trying to test these. Nigga please I make cheese, I know you know better then to fuck with a nigga with nuts as swole as these, you might as well open up yo mouthpiece and suck on these, I know you know better then to fuck with Gee's like these, nigga please.

If you want some come get some. I got something for that ass willing and waiting with the 45 special waiting to blast. Yo life won't last, do a nigga end and smoke him like a blunt to pass, as I stand to deliver, hit a nigga with the lead and make his body shake and shiver hit em from the head to the liver, nigga I stand to deliver a full clip a put you face down in the dust, I tote guns to bust walking on dust for funds we list, I get down with the get down, its just me and my 45 don't fuck with us, I aim to bust, lay down and stay down after catching round after round, I ain't got time to play around if you gone do it, do it to it, and ain't never had a problem with blowing right through it, nigga please don't fuck with these. You should know better then to fuck with niggas with nuts as swole as these nigga please, you got me fucked up, don't fuck with these. I though you knew better then to fuck with Gee's like these, nigga please.

I'M FROM A PLACE

I'm from the land where niggas cook hard water make it boil up, simer down cool it off, dry it off, break it up, bag it up, and then pass it around I'm from the town, the big O where Raiders belong, the place where hustla smoke bomb till it's gone, slanging hardballs until their all gone, where real niggas get killed in the streets and life goes on. I'm from a place where it ain't nothing wrong with giving DA block a good push, the place where can find a connect everywhere you look I'm from a place where the G's and OG's get down, and you ain't doing it right unless you representing the town, the land of milk and honey, the place where the bass makes the earth shake, from place where niggas fall in love with the taste of the OG cush, day to day grinding give the daily push. The Big O where niggas get down, all about the mighty dollar, making these bitches holla, making them bring that money back, one of the homes of the ho stole where pockets, and pimp hands can get out of control, I'm from a place where niggas stay on the hunt for cash, looking for bigger and better things to make that fast cash last, a place where niggas die for nothing because we use to struggling, a place where a gun fight is nothing, I'm from a place where haters stay out to get you ready to rob anybody and everybody standing with you. The O where some niggas don't even jump off the highway, so if you smell like pussy don't even come my way, the place where niggas get caught up everyday, the place where you can hear the sounds of gun spray everyday. The land of hard hitter, wig splitters, dope dealers, and go getters, where fake niggas can't afford to ride with us. The place where the black panthers were invented, armed and deadly, fuck dangerous we were taught to shoot first and aim to bust. Can't afford to die when you fuck with us, I'm from a place where niggas stay down to bust and aim to touch, where life is potentially dangerous, I'm forever representing the yea area I thought you knew, where real pimps, playas, hustlers, killas, dope dealers, and wig splitter to make money like we're suppose too where most niggas, live a life they can't afford to show you, you might steal from me and I might have to fold you, I'm from a place, of killas, hard hitters, dope dealers, and wig splitters like I told you, where niggas quick to give you a clip, like they owed you, the soft can't afford to come through. So if you smell like pussy don't even bother to come through, a place where if you get caught slipping even the police might kill you, where life is all about that all mighty doller and respect is what matters most, thinking of ways to make fast cash last longer, and the favorite pass time is cooking hard water. I'm from a place.

Rewrite both part 1 and 2

I'M A PIMP
PART 1

Shit I should have pimped myself, I gotta head of myself, diping in trying to get in, where I fit in, never try to turn a ho into a housewife because that's when these hos start hoing, back in the day I wasn't knowing dame where is this ho going, dame yall niggas ain't knowing, just because the bitch opened up and gobbled dick for me, doesn't mean the bitch was meant for me, that bitch ain't did shit for me, any bitch and can gobble and swallow, but can a bitch bring that money back after she sucks and swallow, now its pimping bitch follow, have that bitch out here putting her lips on everything around like a drunk with a bottle, the bitch head got too big, she thought she was a super model, if you ask me she was meant to swallow, bitch don't talk just follow, I'm All American I can be yo hero if you want me to be, as long as you bring that money back I will be all I can be, its pimping all American you can fuck, suck, spit or swallow it really don't matter to me, I'm sick of these fake ass bitch slut up bitch and bring that money to me, pimp hand as far as the eye can see, what else am I suppose to do to a bitch that tried to down me, can't let this bitch take my manhood and control me shut up bitch because you owe me, she's my little private pocket pussy for profit, once she starts she ain't stopping, she got miles to go, with a mouth like that they got to know, she knows when to come and she knows when to go. Like a pimp told me its a cold world and I don't love these hos and remember a pro said so I need my money back so you gets to go, to the nearest ho stroke available so I can profit, don't worry about the money I get I keep the money in the pocket, never let a bitch try to get you, bitch why you think I pimp you, you just a scandalous ass bitch now tell that nigga to come get you, and bring that cash to me, all that money belongs to me, pimp hand stronger than the eye can see, I'm pimping out here never let a bitch pimp me money makes the world go round, regulars come back because they get addicted to that sucking sound, bitch I'm a pimp just to make it understood. I know this bitch would try to get me if she could, but as long as she brings that money home to daddy bitch its all good just to make it understood.

PART 2

I'm a pimp bitch suck and swallow bitch popping pussy more then she pop bottles I'm a pimp, so bitch bring that money home to daddy and once you start you can't stop, just give them what they ask for until the pop I'm a pimp, pimp hand stronger then I'm suppose to, keeping these ho's in line pimping these bitches like I'm suppose to bring that money home to daddy bitch because I told you bitch I'm a pimp. She makes it feel so good. I'm the pimp and yo the ho just to make it understood I'm a pimp, you fake bitch I show you, you hoing because I told you, let them niggas know too I'm a pimp, and this bitch makes it feel so good. Just stick to the script bitch and its all good pimp hand stronger then the eye can see. I'm out to get the cash bitch if you a ho then follow me. I'm a pimp, she can sucky sucky long time, if you got enough money you can keep her she ain't my bottom dime, I just want the mind and the money, you can keep the body that's fine, don't worry about me I'm just pimply this old bitch of mine, I'm a pimp, pimping like I told you for the right price it ain't nothing she won't do for you. She'll suck and swallow just like I told you, and gobble you up just like she owed you I'm a pimp, ain't no time to love these has give me mine and me fine, loving this pimp hand of mine, bitch because I'm a pimp, doing what pimps do, if you don't know what to do with yo life then bitch let me pimp you, I'm a pimp, she'll make you feel so good, she'll open up and swallow dick just like she said, as long as she brings the money home to daddy, then ho its all good, because I'm a pimp, pimpping harder than I'm suppose, bitch don't make me tell you again bring that money to daddy like I told you, bitch I'm a pimp.

THE FAST LANE

What do you do in a situation you can't control, do you hold on to life or do you just let go, caught up in the fast lane living a life where its hard to say no, do I hold on or do I just let go, why do I say yes when I should just say no, where did my common cents go, always saying yes when I should just say no. Caught up in the fast lane, I ain't got nothing to prove, with everything to loose, paying the price for living the hard life, never scared to die the hard way, in the land of AK nines and Mossberg pumps with the pistal grip, the land of no mercy, where niggas die to protect they grip, you get got if you slip, out here standing on my own two, I gotta keep my balance before I start to slip too, I can't let my mental state trip, I know their dying to catch me slip, holding on before its time to let go, out here where its all or nothing, niggas known for busting, to afraid not to hold back. I'm protecting me and mines I can't afford to leave my nut sac behind, out here where an easy life is hard to find, haters beware, if you know how it feels to walk in my shoes, then you know how hard it is to live out here, living a life you can't control do you hold on, or do you just let go, niggas die for less, out here where 45's stay cocked and aimed at the chest to ease the stress, with no money and no remorse for those that fell, living in this world were we were born to raise hell, living a life of do dirt and can't tell shit I might as well sell, to me there's worse things in life then going to hell, living a life where we were born to fell, surrounded by hustlers, playas, pimps who do dirt and can't tell, I think you can survive anywhere if you were born in hell, it's never hard to fail, so why would you set a nigga up to fail, trying to hold on to life. Like I'm suppose to no matter what I go through life is hard, and then we die, I'm just trying to hold on to that twinkle in my eye, they call life a bitch and now I know why stuck in the belly of the beast where we do dirt and can't tell dying inside and you can't tell, caught up in the fast lane so I sell shhh don't tell, how much deeper can I go if we're already living in hell, trying to keep my balance before I catch a bullet to the brain, hoping my life ain't for nothing, scared but I don't say nothing, I just hope they don't catch me naked out here look at my life and I'm still out here, holding my 45 scared to let go, why do I say yes when I should just say no I wonder if I should cockback and bust him, putting my faith in GOD even though I don't trust him, I'm tried of being sick and tired, squeeze a few off in the sky just to say fuck em its hard to put your life in the hands of GOD when you don't trust him, hoping my life ain't for nothing even though I feel like I'm good for nothing, stuck in the fast lane where niggas die for nothing, out here in these streets trying to make something out of nothing, stuck in this life where niggas die for nothing, trying to hold on before I let go why do I say yes when I should just say no, sometimes I wonder if I should just let go.

AFTER I ZIP UP

That bitch ain't my bottom dime, around here pussy is pussy and money is the bottom line, cash before hos, stop wasting my time, pussy is pussy, pussy ass nigga that's why I stay stuck to the grind, that bitch ain't my bottom dime when I want to get sucked up I'll keep that bitch in mind, can't let these hos get ahead of themselves, that bitch ain't mine, you can have the bitch that's fine, even when she was mine, she wasn't mine, I'm too focused on the grind but if I wanted her to suck me up, I know she'd do just fine, you can keep the body, sometimes I just mesmerise the mind, if you want the bitch after I zip up. I know she'll do just fine, handcuffing hos is bad for my health, after you finish with the bitch, put the bitch back on the shelf, that bitch ain't my bottom dime; I keep hos on deck and these bitches in line, I stay stuck to the grind, so get yo feeling straight, I'm straight fuck these bitches and don't hate, stop wasting my time, fuck these hand me down hos, I'm all about me and mine, me and my money will be just fine, pick up after I zip up and homie she'll do just fine, and when I'm finish I'll keep that number in mind, get mad that's fine, just don't hate on mine, that bitch ain't my bottom dime, just keep that in mind she's my little something, something whenever I find time, after I zip up you can have the bitch, because its back to the grind, ain't no need to hate on mine, when I'm finish with the bitch, I put that bitch on line, so stop hating on my mine, as soon as I'm finish she'll call you and do just fine, pussy is pussy and her pussy ain't mine, I'm too focused on the grind. I'm the nigga that complament the bitch and tell her she sitting on a gold mine, just don't fuck up and hate on mine you can have the bitch as soon as I zip up mine, I'm sure she'll do just fine, as soon as you finish with the bitch, put the bitch back on line. Ain't no time to worry about these hand me down ho's, I stay mesmerised by the grind, time is money so don't waste mine you can keep the bitch in yo back pocket me, and money will be just fine. Pussy is pussy and her pussy ain't mine.

So stop worrying about mine, that bitch ain't my bottom dime, you can have the bitch back as soon as I zip up mine, money is the bottom line, cash before ho's just keep that in mind, so do what you do screw what you screw, and stop hating on mine, that bitch ain't my bottom dime, I know she sitting on a gold mine but her pussy ain't mine, you can have her as soon as I zip up mine, I ain't worried about the bitch, the bitch ain't mine, so stop hating on mine, you suppose to keep the bitch on line, but shhh don't hate on mine that bitch ain't mine I too busy stuck to the grind, you can have the bitch back as soon as I zip up mine, man that bitch ain't mine so stop hating on mine, bitches ain't hard to find that's why I stay focused on the grind. Pussy is pussy loving to see her pussy sucks up mine, time after time I'll tell you that bitch ain't mine, cash before hos keeping that money on line, you can have the bitch back as soon as I zip up mine. I'm sure as soon as she's done with me she'll do just fine, just remember when your finish put that bitch back on line, so I can zip up mine.

HEART TO THE STREET

Mo money, mo problems that's what they told me, can't trust nobody that's what life showed me, out here to collect what life owes me these haters ain't got no loyalty for me, it's just me and only me putting the heat to the street, taking care of myself putting money in my pocket like a grown man suppose to, I gotta get mine I could give a fuck about yours, I went out to get it, couldn't afford to split it came back and Saran wrapped it up, letting my talking do the walking, out here, just sticking to the groove, I'm a hustla making the block move, talk ain't cheap, back and forth to the spot about three times a week, can't let the block get weak, I'm an out of the ordinary hustla my price you can't be beat, send the bass to yo seat all you gotta do is let it sink in, it's time to reap I got money to send, with all these haters praying for my downfall, yall niggas fake I'd rather count money then fuck with ya'll, sitting on a grip, nigga my pockets stand tall, yall niggas love to hate on me that's why I don't fuck with ya'll.

Surviving in the game, sticking to the game plan so I don't fall, I can see the hate in the haters eyes praying for my downfall, so fuck ya'll, I'm out here to my a grip, until it's time to take another trip, Momma I'm balling, I hope my pockets don't rip, slanging zip for zip, playa potna don't trip, I can lower the price as soon I take another trip I gotta get mine you gotta get yours, I'm just the nigga to make sure you get what you paid for. Talk ain't cheap, I'm hustling back and forth about two or three times a week, striking to the groove I'm a hustla even with my life on the line, I gotta make the block move, loving every time I touch down. They say its hell or jail when your taking penatentry chances, I need my cash up cash homie no first hand advances, I can't afford to take chances I'm out here in these streets making moves for advancement, out here dying to win, sitting on a stack of cash as the world spins, putting work in actions speak louder the words I need more then a nine to five, that's why I kick it with bosses that kick birds my nigga fuck what you heard.

I could give a fuck what you say I'm out here making a DA Block move almost everyday, until my pockets turn gray, making my fast cash last longer, them niggas round the block hate me because my game plan was stronger nigga I'm just doing what it do, I'm here to get mine so fuck you, I think BIG I don't wantta be as small time as you if it don't make dollars it don't make cents. I want more then the rent, keeping track of every doller spent. I got cash in my pocket, no more days of lint, keeping track of penny every dollar, and every cent, I gotta get paid, with my hand on something low kye in case these niggas act shade, out here putting the heat to street, making moves back and forth two or three times a week, holla at yo playa potna I got a price you can't beat. I'm making DA Block move putting that heat to the street.

WHO CAN YOU REALLY TRUST

Who can you really trust, now that the worlds a battlefield we lust to bust holding steal, engaged in combat with my iron and iron will, we don't live life for the thrill no more, no more open door, no more living life without my fourty four, what happened to life what happen to death before dishonor, stuck in the trenches leading the lambs to the slautter, now a days they don't even respect loyalty and honor what happen to the rules and regulation to the game, these ole money hungery ass niggas with their hands out begging for change, if you ask me they don't even belong in the game, its step on or be stepped on, ain't no love no more, ain't no days and hugs no more, why would you waste time, its a war out there and I'm getting mine sticking to the game plan steady stuck to the grind, ain't worried about these haters, they'll show their ass in due time, until then I'm on the hunt for mine, they say give me got shot in the back of the head and so did Ted and Fred, and the rest of them niggas born dead I don't fuck with them niggas, I only fuck with the real, born and raised in the battlefield where niggas don't play, they shoot to kill, who can I trust when we all lust to bust, its fuck yall, if yall ain't down with us, I'm stuck in the trenches I squeeze with no fuss, you can look but don't touch, chrome tight making sure these niggas don't do too much. We all want the same thing, the money, the women, power, respect and the American Dream, but you can't trust a backstabber, so I'm kicking all them fake niggas off the team, one by one, until they buy one from me, they said it ain't no rules no more, it's all about currency, so I'm getting mine with a twist of lime holding onto my chrome two, protecting mine, we all want the same thing and I put in work so I'd be dame if I let a nigga come and take mine you can't trust these niggas as far as you can throw em, grew up with some of these niggas and I don't even know em, I don't know what happen. I'm real I showed em, by the way the stacks added up I thought I told em, no love for them niggas, no love at all, holding on to a niggas legs hoping I fall, I got too many enemies I have no need for yall, living in the Lion Den where its eat or be eatten, these fake niggas talk shit but the real ain't speakin, speakin words unsaid, because actions speak louder then words, I only kick it with the chosen few like I'm suppose to do me and my chrome two, who can you trust when we all lust to bust, I don't need a nigga I can't trust, I don't need a fake bitch I can't touch, and I don't need chrome I can't bust. I can't fuck with yall niggas, because yall ain't down with us. Fucking with them niggas is like standing under a fallin trees I ain't taking no chances them niggas might try to put an end to me hit me, and I got enough against me, like I said before you either with me or against me, if you ain't with me, you could be the nigga sent to hit me, that's why I keep my chrome two with me for them niggas that ride against me. The worlds a battlefield you won't survive if you let shit slid, bring it to them niggas and let em know what time it is, if you down with us, you might have to bust, most of these niggas fake, but I'm real and a fake nigga you can't trust, I'm real and the real ain't going nowhere, I'm out here standing on my own too, too real to trust you, you need chill then come through, I won't except nothing but cash from you. I'm real because I'm suppose to be no love for these fake niggas with no love for me, only let these niggas see what they suppose to see, ain't no fake in me. I'm as real as I can be, it ain't no changing me, even if you try to slip me up and rearrange me, I might bend, but the strongest couldn't break me, that fake shit probable rubbed off on them but never me, who can you really trust when we all lust to bust, ready to let the chrome touch, the niggas I know deadly we passed dangerous ain't no nigga gone look out for me, like me myself and I stuck in trenches until the day I die, hearing in the grind and we all know why. I only trust a few, I can't lie, making as much as I can until its time to kiss this life goodbye, why aim low when you can aim high, watch yo head nigga, we all want a pie of the pie.

HIT EM UP

Hit em, hit em, hit em, hit em, hit em up, we do dirt then we up, I brought the AK to fuck around, lovin the way the clip sound; bustin round after round, getting down just to get down get hit, its a guarantee you would be found, we spit fire to light up your life, and never ever think twice, - here put an end to life, it won't lock up on you if you spin it right put a nigga in the dirt by the end of the night, now tell me what you like, a miles meters, 38, 40, 44, 45, 50 cals, AK AR HK how about a SKS to light up yo chest, for those who chose to test the technique, take a dirt knap, putting these nigga to sleep, put these niggas in they place before they try to creep; opportunity is all I seek, I'm a bonified hustler ain't no fucking with me. I hold on to a itch trigger finger ready to bust continually. You can have it however you like, it really don't matter to me. I'm more then all. I can be, why can't you see, if you got a problem with me potna then you bring it to me, these fake motherfuckers get no love from me.

Penitentiary

KILLA SHIT

They hate me because I talk about hustlers, killin and drug dealing, stackin money to the cillan for the feelin, parking lot pimping reeling them in fillin them in, Boss Bossin it blowing smoke in the wind. Yeah I know why they love to hate, and why they try to break me because I'm real like I'm suppose to be, that's why these niggas ain't folding me I was born and raised on the block, where niggas hustle, and get shot where real niggas get caught up and spend time in the penn a lot, we all out here on a mission for the top, weather you like it or not, the water's too deep we can't stop, its either sink or swimming. I'm talking to these motivated money makers like me built to win in this world of full clips and sin heartache and getto grins, watching out for them haters as the rims spin, creeping on the way up, enough is never enough. I want mo money mo money mo money mo for show, holla at yo playa potna and I'll give you what you ask for. I'm just a doller away, for these niggas dying to pay, its just another dollar, another day in the life I live, I know they hate me for living but this is how I live, with so much negativity its so hard to be positive but this is the life I live, hard time for hard crimes, stackin chips blowing dank under the sunshine, on a mission to get paid, get laid and stack until my world is mine, if I grind hard enough happiness will come in due time, stuck in this world of mine, doing it until the job is done these haters chasing me like the moon chases the sun, always on the move and on the run from the gun holding the bullet with my name on it, I've seen fate and it ain't no way I can run from it, so I stand to stand and deliver to protect mine before they take mine, stomp or be stomped on they out to take all I own, you can't stand hand to hand with my chrome hoping these haters do something besides hate on me, I talk about life and what's real, you can't buy the fake shit here. No bullshit allowed I why I loosen the crowd, if you go anything to say make sure you speak up loud, the truth hurts and you know it, I ain't the only one to show it. I put the pen to the pad and flow it, its hard for a Boss out here and you know it, whether you believe it or not, out to stack a knott. Mr. Stack a lot, watching for that infa red dot ready to take my spot. Hoping to get blessed by the Lord above, fuck these hating ass niggas they get no love, in this life of push and shove, backstabbers, heartacks, and meanmugs, the hate on my financial growth and the life I live that's why they gets no love from me only pounds of green, opium, and snow from me, out here being all I can be, until they lock me up or put an end to me, now what don't you see. I stay as real as real can be, until the end of me, until they lock me up and throw away the key with nothing but hard time and commissary, in this life of stress and strife ain't nothing nice but that's life, can win it all or watch it all fall with one roll of the dice, out here paying the price to live life, I can see these haters hating and all eyes on me, they don't know the do's and don'ts and its plain to see, none of these motherfuckers can ever be like me, stuck in the game on full blast in love with fast cash, fast cars and beautiful women as far as the eye can see, ain't another nigga out here as real as me and they hate me because I'm all about hustlin, killin and drug dealin, stack in money to the cillian for the feelin, parking lot pimping reeling them in fillin them in, a Boss Bossin it blown smoke in the wind. I do this shit for real, no time to pretend, time is money playa potna holla back when you got money to spend, fuck these hating if its about money I'm all in, sliding around DA Block letting my tires spin. This is the game and I'm in, heating up the block smoking dame I'm hot again, club to the spot again, dusting these haters off again.

(GREAT LYRICS + GREAT BEAT + GREAT DELIVERY) = GREAT SONG

I another Boss in it, another haust in it, sliding in the underbucket don't you see me flossing it, holla at yo homeboy and show us all you get, you see my life I'm flossin it. This is the game and until death I'm in it to win it all, I want it all git and grinding even after I fall, I got to have until my money stands tall, I can't stop even after I get the Benz drop I want the top I can't stop, I can't stop flowing letting DA Block know who got it for the low. When I do dirt I ride low, remember at all times its all about the dough, money makes the world go round from my town to yo town as the wheels spins, in the grind its about money I'm all in, putting these haters in the wind, no time to pretend, staying as real as real can get, remembering every bitch I hit, every bullet I spit, money for snow money is all I get, putting my town in the air letting you know who I'm with, if you hate then hate is all you get, if you down with the hustle then stay down with it put yo hustle to the grind keep that money on yo mind you gotta grind before you shine, just keep stepping the dough will come in due time, shaking these haters off my mind, mind over muscle steady stuck in the struggle I can't do shit but hustle, I was told no money no trouble, hard time for hard crime living this life with more grit then grime, hard crime and hustles to shine out here you gotta be about yo dough, this money and I'm all about mine, I invest in dough before shine, pushing hard time to the back of my mind, this is the game and I'm about mine, here to get what's mine, sticking to the script I'll reach the top in due time, here until they take or break mine, I'm a Boss in it, another haust in in, sliding in the underbucket don't you see me flossing it I'm on the grind to get mine 2 for 15 is all you get, they looking for another Boss in it, another haust in it, sliding in the under bucket don't you see me flossin it, holla at yo boy snow is all you get, transactions I'm down with it.

I don't know what I'd do without my Chevy every time I slide bye, I'm sitting heavy.

MILLION DOLLER HIT

[If you ain't with me yous against me, one of these motherfuckas tried to million doller hit me. If you ain't with me yous against me, these niggas the reason why I keep my strap with me, if you ain't with me yous against if I gots to die these niggas dying with me.]

Its me and mine against the world. They want my mind body and soul trying to leave my brain scattered on the concrete, but I refuse to meet defeat when they turn up the beef, is when I bring out the heat, loaded and cocked at all times, its too many haters in the air you can smell the bullshit from a mile away, in this life of hard crime and hard time left with hate and this piece of mine, I could die any day, you either with me or against. That's all I'll say before I commence with the gun spray, stuck in the trenches with a price on my head totting lead they said I'm better off dead, these niggas must have forgotten who they fucking with. I'm as real as real gets, I tote iron to spit, no time to play around when its life or death, when its time to for beef I'm squeezing off every last metalic piece from my piece, ready to unload the beast in these streets. No mercy, no prisoner, no pussy allowed, these niggas want beef so I came to bust rounds, you know how I get down, without a word said its off with yo head, them niggas hate for nothing so they better off dead. I keep my ear to the street, heard about the beef through the grapevine, brought the military issue to take mine, these niggas ain't as cold as I, when the shit hits the fan, its overtime, I'm the nigga you tried to hit, I'm a nigga with more gitt and grimme living with my piece of pistal to protect what's mine, I don't bark, I'll let clip speak for me, actions speak louder then words, so what it is, nigga do what you do, its about that time for me and mines to slide through, getting rid of these niggas like waste management, these niggas wanted my head but a full clip is all you get. You'll know when I pull out and aim to spit, these niggas put a price on my head, but death is all you get. Must I remind these niggas who they fucking with. I'm the nigga about dollars and cents, sitting low key with my strap on deck, out here to maxi pad these niggas out here softer then Kotex, protecting my set with my piece with the beast, if them niggas knew better they'd keep my name out the streets, I see no evil but I hear it all the motherfucking time, prepared for anything at anytime these niggas trying to divide my face and take my throne, I don't take threats lightly so I live with my chrome, don't show you face around me, you likely to catch a full clip to the dome, if you want some I got something for that ass, I fuck with hustlas, killas, dope dealers fast cars, and fast cash, if you ain't with me then yous against me if I gots to die, them niggas dying with me, if you want me come and get me, I'm no pussy I ain't going nowhere, fuck you and yo million doller hit, these niggas want me dead but a body full of lead is all you get, you wasted yo money I had to cancel yo hit, had to remind these niggas, to let them know who they fucking with. I hope these niggas remember the taste when your getting yo mind earsed. I'm laced with game. I'm the nigga calling you out to split yo frame, no guts no glory nigga, why would I worry about yo million doller hit, when I got a million doller clip to deliver, I protect the tech and technique, I roll with the best, I wouldn't settle for less, dust to dust ashes to ashes GOD bless, one nigga less no time for stress. I want it done to them like it was done to me. I won't settle for less collecting stripes in this bitch, me and my million doller mouthpiece holding on to the beast until the time to release, its closing time holding my piece until the violence seize.

REWRITE REWRITE REWRITE

Moving do ain't to shine, risking penitentiary time for hard crimes, I'm a money motivated hustla I'm all about the grind. I'm here to get mine with the smell of money on my mind, if I just stick to the game plan I'll be touching the top in no time. Good things come to those who wait, and I've been waiting a long time, now I'm here to take or break mine I'm smart about the hustle, I put up before they get a chance to take mine, I'm strong in the mind, I may stumble but I won't fall, even with the weight of the world on my shoulders I won't break, even with the stress and strain that rotts my brain, I take the pain of life grit my teeth and maintain, the stress is in your brain money, muscle, and mind over matter, I push most of the bullshit to the side when we're gone the bullshit won't matter, sticking to the routine to make my pockets grow. I'll do almost anything for the dough, from hitting licks to moving the snow, ask them boys about me, when it was some dirt to be done, it was hardly done without me I stay real ain't no reason to doubt me, sticking to the game plan until I get caught up or these niggas out me, sometimes I put my soul on hold. I need money now I can't wait until I'm old, I need something to hold on to I can't even remember the big faces I blow throw, just like you I want it all, so I can kick back relax in the shade drink some ice cold lemonade and hit the badest bitch with her back against the wall. Tell her I want it all my dick stands tall. I do dirt and move work, we hustle until we fall, hoping there's something soft to land on, I'm just a soldier in these trenches getting my cash on, I don't want to be if I should I would get my blast on, no time for these haters. I busy getting my cash on, as life goes on, listening to the same fat bitch singing the same old song trying to end my game and carry me home, but we all know I ain't in the struggle all on my own, it ain't nothing new to me life goes on, hitting different bitches with different thongs, always remember nothing goes right unless you keep yo money strong, money over bitches, that bitch is just a bitch in a thong my life goes on, stuck in the struggle so you know I carry on, snow for dough. Praying no hate comes my way I'm making cash, trying to make it last longer then before, my game triumph stronger then before, just another day another dollars yeah I know, I know, its all been done before, just putting the pieces of the puzzle together again, kicking birds of the feather again, you know yo playa potna its always whatever again if ain't nothing change we can ride together again. I'm just a pusha man moving that weather again, on top sliding through the struggle again, getting that cash first, my pockets hurt when I hit the block without work, watching out for them boys they always the first to blast, that why I stay low key, doing my do dirt on the low hoping they don't find me, I'm here whenever, just pick up to find me living with more problems, then money, the grind ain't nothing but hard times and fast money, now I'm on to bigger and better things, now I want more then shine. I can't make money serving penitentiary time. It's time to use that money brain to maintain, stepping up in this rap game, upgrading the game, I can't afford to get caught slipping I got too much to lose to be out here set tripping, I'm rearranging my grind so long hard time and penitentiary time. I'm too bright not to shine, figuring out the road of success, to ease my stress, I want the top and nothing less, come fuck with yo boy. I'm still the same, just upgraded the game surpassing the dope game, the grind has changed, just pick up to find me, I got a couple boxes ready to roll sitting beside me. If you do do dirt on the low make sure them boys don't know, I out here doing my thing holla at yo playa potna, whenever, I got a pound to blow, I'll be here until its time to go.

THE END OF ME

I'm real and they just pretend to be, they want to see the end of me, lock me up threw away the key and put an end to me. I'm real and they just pretend to be, they want to see the end of me, man you should have seen their faces after they sentenced me, they plan to put an end to me. I'm not fake and I don't pretend to be, hard time is what they've given me now, they ain't as real as <u>me</u>. If it was up to them they'd lock me up for the whole centu<u>ry</u>, hard time is what they've given me, could this be the end of me. Got caught up living this life of mine hard time for hard crimes, don't tell me you know what I'm going through you can't understand this life of mine, its like they don't even listen to the evidence, it feels like the truth of the matter is no longer irrelevant, they just want me handcuffed and shackled and locked away, until the end of me, it looks like this could be the end for me, looking in the courtroom for family I don't see. I can't get mad I don't have no one to blame but me. When it all went down, somehow it all fell on me, new case new charge with a brand new felony, locked up and locked down, you can hear the chains every time I jail hop around, the sound of your life chained up I got too much to let go, I could never give up. Stuck in these county browns until my time is up, no matter what happen to me I could never ever give up. They plan to put an end to me, its something about being on the inside that makes the outside stop, hoping I can face my fate hoping my heart don't skip a beat, I hope my heart don't drop. I want to fast forward time, but we all know time won't stop, listening to the courtroom clock tic and toc, I'm a real man but I'm scared to watch, listening to them debate my case while I'm chained and locked, sweating bullets every time I hear that hammer knock, hoping the defense attorney missed a spot, so they can unchain the locks, it feels like their trying to put an end to me, chain me up and lock me down for the whole century sounds like hard time is wining me, everybody in the courtroom can plainly see. I'm not the one they want, even though it seems to be your honor please tell the defendant not to afend me, I don't care where they sending me, it don't matter this is the of me they don't care and its plain to see, they ain't as real to me mad I'm not free when I need to be, sounds like it could be the end of me, they want to lock me up and throw away the key but your honor you didn't hear from me, the person that looked like me wasn't me, those fingerprints you got they sent where fake you see, I'm here because they love to hate on me, I'm innocent and its plain to see, you know it ain't no believing me, my lawyers keeps telling I should take the deal that they giving me, now you see, they trying to put an end to me. Chain me up and lock me down for the whole century. This time wasn't meant for me fucking with them niggas, they ain't real <u>but</u> they pretend to be they ain't as real as me, charged with the case that they pened on me, hard time is what they've given me, this could be the end of me, these niggas ain't family, but their quick to pretend to be, them niggas ain't as real as me, even if I'm facing a century when I get out they gotta deal with me, until the end of me I'm doing hard time that wasn't meant for me, they tried to put an end to me, chain me up and lock me down for the whole century them niggas ain't no friend to me, they want to see the end of me, until the of me, I'm real and they pretend to be, doing hard time that wasn't meant for me, hard time for hard crimes was the deal for me. I'm gone this is the end of me. I'm gone for a whole century, this is the end of me, them niggas ain't real but they pretend to be.

THESE NIGGAS DON'T WANT IT WITH ME

You can't touch me boy

You gone need more than the dogs you got to hurt me boy. The word on the street said you want to merk me boy. Yo block turned against ya. These niggas ain't got shit to say when yo homies not with ya. If these niggas ain't with ya they against ya, searching for the right box to fit ya. Hoping these niggas die with ya.

These niggas will get bought and sold fucking with a G like me, you fucking with a nigga not afraid to saw off a sawed off, throwing buck shots to the brain, I'm never ever soft just ask yo bitch maybe then you'll get an ideal of who you really fucking with, I stay hardcore my dick stands at attention when its time for war. I'm hot these niggas better not touch me I'm sick with it. I got it come and get it, these niggas bitch made waring the beef yo bitch made, that's how you know these niggas ain't real, if you know the game, then you know you break the rules right here trying to pump fear when my hearts not here, these niggas can't fuck with me, these niggas you see can never get enough of me. Keeping it in yo ear until these haters get enough of me, these niggas can never be as real as me, these niggas crossed the game, I'm still the same nigga ain't a dame thing change, I took the lost nigga and now its tatted on the brain, rolling with the ups and downs is all apart of the game the word on the street said they wanted to merk me, now which one, is the one who won touch me. Make these niggas sit down and shut up, don't you hear a grown man talking, it really don't matter to me either run up, gun up or get stepping my nuts not for testing, introduce these niggas to the sandman lay them down and put them to sleep, these niggas should think better before they insult me, they just throw gas on the fire, nigga I'm use to the heat, them niggas caught me naked in the street and I didn't miss a beat, ain't no pussy over here unless you won get fucked, have that nigga swimming up shit creek with no boat and no luck, and they want me face down in the mud, thinking I ain't ready to go pound for pound nigga slug for slug, I got something steal for yo grill and yo mean mug, I could give two fucks about yo two face, nigga I smoke mine with no lace. I think about the pen everytime I see yo face knowing what lies inside these niggas try to hide, ready to put a hole through a nigga from outside to inside, when the shit hit the fan I'm the nigga that never tried to hide, face to face with my fate, these niggas need to stop talking shit before its way too late, nigga you better tell yo boy. Where I'm from niggas don't play around when they pull out and aim the toy, these fully metal jackets ain't a game to me. These niggas crossed the game and now they want to merk me, send them niggas to the belly of the beast, and watch them niggas bitch up when I turn up the heat, have them niggas pissing in they seat for trying to test my testees, I bet you never met cold hearted niggas like this. These niggas ain't no major deal, pimp slap these niggas and tell em to suck on these when you roll with the big dogs you don't fuck with fleas, these niggas ain't shit to be but a motherfucking felony I'm hot to death, dare a nigga to come touch me, have these niggas spitting up dirt permanently. I'll tell these niggas one more time, nigga don't fuck with me.

These niggas want to merk me
only GOD ran hurt me, standing
on my own two until I can't
stand, I ain't scared of no man
I'm living to die, putting my life
in GOD's hands

LOCK N KEY

Can't you see we own DA Block, ball and chain in the dope game, with the key to the lock, when you do what we do you gotta keep the street on lock holding the key to the city. Fish scale is so pretty, 100% raw and uncut, dealing with the real deal, you know fish scale will is known to give you that superman feel rolling with the A.C.T we something like the A.D.T just follow yo nose if you want some of that T.N.T, homie we gotta eat, around here we pay to play, up with no sleep, chopper in the cuts waiting for them niggas who try to creap, check the price tag potna, got that price you can't beat, and with this right here they'll be jumping out they seat, got it on hand 24 7 7 days a week, no bullshit around that fake shit ain't found here I'll say it again that raw an uncut just to make that shit clear so if it ain't about business stay the fuck from round here, we do it bigger then most, on the highways and buy ways from coast to coast, go head and tell them who you love the most. The A.C.T you know where to find me holding the lock and key to the game making it simple and plain. We want it all, once you grow up you can't fall unlock the chain and ball, outsiders can't come around, these niggas don't play around, if you know business, you know how we fuck around, we lay it down, where ever its found, keeping my snowshoes on every time winter comes around, you know how we get down, you play where you stay, at the work house day after day, potential hard time for hard crimes you know how we play, waters run deep be careful before you drown these niggas don't fuck around, when your down you stay down, when ever your in a clench holla at the potna before you drown, I stay down especially when hard time comes around, these new comers to the game don't come around because of how we get-down, fucking with the A.C.T. ain't no time to fuck around, where here to lay it down we gotta eat ain't no time to fuck around, we only fucking with the best, when in doubt we test and nothing less, the best of the best, I thought I told yall fuck boys before don't ever ever come around here unless you want some more. We got the best for show, you ain't heard if you got the money playa potna we can fly bird for bird that's the word, we keep it playa potna fuck what you heard, we play for keeps, we own the streets. Its time to get in where you fit in, we up with no sleep, open 24 7, 7 days a week if its that cream you seek, just follow yo nose trust me my shit ain't weak, <u>when they look to up</u>, <u>they look for mine to beat</u>. I got heat here goes a little guarantee, to keep them out they seat, just follow your nose if its cream you seek we hold the lock and key, come fuck with the A.C.T., owners of the block, here to keep these niggas in line and these streets on lock, that raw and uncut simple and plain, come fuck with us when you want to numb your brain.

DA STREETS

X2

We ride in da streets, we slide in da streets, meet my fate face to face these niggas can't hide in da streets, they lie in da streets, we die in da streets, we close range aim hit em up high in da streets.

Who want to ride with me slide with, when its time to hit em up high ride with me, you gotta be one of a kind to slide with me in these streets all day until they come and get me, representing DA BLOCK for life, I call the streets my home, remembering even with chrome the realest nigga can die alone living in these streets taking hard time for hard crimes, mixing good luck with bad times, to me its just another day another doller in this life of mine, here until I'm gone, the streets my only place to roam, riding in these streets in love with my 44 riding sitting back low in case they blow through my <u>door</u> life ain't nothing nice, you never know which way the winds blow, I could die tonight its all been done <u>before</u>, no guts no glory no balls then no gain, another day in these streets living this life insane, these tinted windows ain't enough to guard your brain, sitting heavy in a Chevy in case I gotta hit em high close range, life ain't never guaranteed living life intoxicated with a half pint and a lime bag of weed, sometimes living with the strain of life that's all you need, riding with my chrome on the side of me. My 44 one of a kind you gotta be to ride with me, letting it be known how I get down when I get down, listening to the tires spin, I'm living with hard crime taking chances of hard time I'm all in, fuck this bag of weed my nigga throw it all in but that shit in the wind coasting down DA Block letting da street listen to my tires spin I'm all in with my game face on, no matter how many smiles I see I don't no about you but life ain't always good to me, I can't trust them niggas up the block, them niggas not with me, safely on safety off incase them niggas try to fuck with me, swanging my Chevy like I'm suppose to be, watching the weed smoke holding me I'm in control but the hen's owning me, and I'm so high I could touch the sky, hit the blunt one more time before I have to say goodbye sliding through the streets still pushing back yack. Keeping my eyes open for these niggas that don't know how to act, even if I left DA Block I would always come back to chop it up with the potnas and blaze a fat doshen sac, I'm from these streets and not a nigga can take that, holding on to life until I'm dead and rotting making the most of life incase I'm forgotten, living this life I live some may look down at me for it, but this is how I live. I could be here on second and gone the next, I'm a rider holding on chrome and every last breath, living life to death, running in these streets were we all compete, doing what I'm suppose to do playa potna making these ends meet, sitting on chrome feet ready to kiss this hen goodbye, before I pour some out for my potnas I need to hit it one last time, life ain't nothing nice living this life of mine, this life of crime do dirt hard crime and hard time, do what you do playa potna, don't change your life for mine, I live in these streets until I die in these streets clutching my heat, hoping I'm not forgotten when I'm gone, after living a life you ain't beat, running down the block listening to the sound of the beat, in love with my 44 we only have one life to live I wonder how much I have left to go I hope I don't have to hit em up high like I said before, but living this life of mine I never know, it's time to tell this hen bottle its time to go, riding through these streets with one life to GO, you can catch me in these streets until its time to GO.

I REMEMBER WHEN THE WORLD MADE CENTS

I remember when the world made cents, trying to make a doller out of fifteen cents, living in a world that got flipped upside down. I don't remember if I'm standing right side up. Sometimes I feel like I'm climbing to the bottom on my way up, am I moving to slow or am I running through life to fast every time I blink my eyes I see life flip the hour glass, trying to figure out why I feel like apart of my past why does life move so fast I can see my life float away in the bottom of every glass, in every puff of smoke, when I inhale and choke, pardon me that's just life stuffing time down my throat, sometimes I feel seasick without a wave or boat feeling my life slip away, hoping to snap out of this daze any day now, one of those day where no matter what I do, I just can't wake up, sleep walking through life trying my best to stay up falling over every obstacle to come my way, don't mind me my life is like this every day, getting pushed around by the forever present ups and downs, looking for piece of mind and some friendly common ground, with none to be found, I'll be here standing over my feet let me know when my life is found, staring at my life through a dirty shot glass outside looking in pouring my life on the pad, they say the truth hurts and my pen never felt so sad, everything's inside out what happen to the life I had, today I feel like wearing my heart on the outside to see how many breaks I get, bartender you're telling me for four doller and fifteen cents a shot is all I get, do you know how much life I spent, dame I guess this shot is all I get so I might as well make the best of it, one more shot down the head and once its gone, I will never come back, falling over my own two feet, my head is so high I can't seem to see across the street but I know its there, I've been there before running through life with my eyes a blur. I think I feel worse then I did before, there goes my pen again get ready for a down pour, dame I remember when life made cents trying to make a doller out of fifteen cents, now I can barely pay the rent, trying to stay focus until I can afford to fall out. I think that was change that fell out my mouth, maybe that was my fifteen cent, maybe I can use that to buy my life back so it all makes cents, maybe I should just keep my mouth shut, falling over my life triping over my own two, I'll be OK, I be OK. I told you all I need is time, don't mind me I'm just running through this life of mine, yeah I'll be just fine I'll be back on my own two in no time, I'm just searching for some peace of mind, once I find some I'll be just fine, just running through this life of mine everything OK. Once I wake up I be just fine writing on this pad with this pen of mine, maybe with this fifteen cents I can buy back this life of mine, now everything just fine don't mind me I'm just trying to leave this shot of mine.

MR. TRIGGER MAN

Reeling in the line, stuck to the grind, I'm the pusher man yo dirty money will spend just fine. Money is the bottom line just don't waste my time out here fucking around with these niggas doing business as usual, when your the pusha man backstabing niggas ain't unusual, pressed for time, time is money when conducting business make sure you read between the lines, taking penitentiary chances, getting hard time for hard crimes, eyes open at all times looking out for those who drop dimes, staring at killas in the shape of dope dealers with itchy trigger fingers, me and my trigger man in hand to make sure the deal goes right, these niggas looking at me funny and my clip has an appetite no bark just bite. As long as everything goes according to plan I won't have to light up yo life, exchanging snow for dough at the same time. Something tells me not to trust these niggas while I got my hand on mine, thinking to myself money is the bottom line, let's finish with this bullshit before these niggas plot and try to take mine, out here fucking with cut throats but business is business everything is going according to plan these niggas and your pusha man with my trigger man in hand, ain't nothing going wrong but these niggas smell fishy to me, if its a lick these niggas want their going to see the ugly side of me, what will be shall be, everything cool my nigga as long as these niggas don't try to fuck me, with all the enemies I got I don't need friends. I'm a hustla to the heart I'm on the grind to the end, fucking around with these niggas that kill for real no time to pretend, got my game face on from beginning to end me and my trusty chrome friend watching every move they make, exchanging snow for dough watching every pack they take. I'm making the money move and everything's running smooth until I see this flash of light they got a hitter in the cuts trying to take my life. I pulled Mr. Trigger Man I didn't think twice. I didn't get burned by the bullet squeezing chrome on these niggas trying to turn heat to ice I'm off with the loot as the guns blow, they want the snow and the dough, over my dead body ducking and dodging with the loot busting at the nigga with the twelve gauge shotre, one down two to go watching out for the nigga who grabed the snow now its two on four, me and my trigger man busting at these niggas as I duck out the door. I reload the clip but not before I hit his hitter man in the hip, trying to keep my head on straight trying to make it to the car before its way too late, listening to lead fly over head waited for the nigga to reload and aimed at his head, jumped in the whip hoping that man's dead, driving away with my head down before they hollow my head, escaped with my loot and my head and left one man dead looked down at my gut and I didn't see red, I had a feeling them niggas was out for my head, alive is better then dead, they came for the snow and the dough and died instead, I'm trying to figure out why I didn't die instead, dame another day another doller to spend looking in my rearview after every block I bend, never do business alone holding my chrome friend, those niggas don't give a fuck the dough and the snow and yo life to end that's why I stick with Mr. Trigger Man my trusty chrome friend, looking in my rearview after every block I bend. I can't believe they wanted my life to end. Now you'll never catch me living without my trusty chrome friend, now I got to go back to the spot with dough to spend. (Dame you'll never believe what just happen to me.)

HOOK

No time for beef out here, don't you see me grinding I ain't tripping off, you my nigga I'm too busy out here shining, staying on my toes potna out here grinding just doing what I do I'm out here hustling potna I thought you knew living with my little piece of pistal, out here doing my thing drinking Henn and Moet living on the California line taking that California lime straight to the kneck, jut living the life I live, no time for beef nigga that's just how I live in, out here doing my thang just living the life I live drinking Gen and Cristal just living my life, living with my little piece of pistal.

POEM

Each step trying to make something out of nothing. Taking the necessary steps to make my goals become reality, taking the necessary steps to make something out of nothing and continue to make progress trying to make things happen whenever thing remains still. Keeping things moving taking the necessary steps to do so living life step by step until I need to step pass what was hoping to become more then what was, staying focused on the task at hand living a life where man eats man, push and pull take without giving where handshake produce heartache and take from those who choose to trust too much living in a world where its kill or die with many lies thrown in between the real and fake, you got to read between the line in this world of give and take, in a world where real chooses to be fake with firm grips and handshakes. A world where people step on the backs of their fellow man just to keep them down just because they can living a world of MAN verses MAN and kill or die where pockets fold up and Bank accounts grow and fall in this world of firm hand shakes suits and ties firm faces with lies that lay in between the lines where people dress to impress and constantly pressed for time stuck in a box fighting over office space with an extra window with an extra foot of space and a deck with the biggest label living in a world where loyalty is nothing more than a fable in a world of suites and ties with lies hidden between the line fighting for the top spot fighting the day the top spot living a life of kill or be killed to reach the top where business never stops living the life of a business man fighting for the top spot for as long as I can I'm a business man doing what I can.

REWIND UNCUT

They're trying to take the life out of me and trying to take the figure out of me and make a bitch out of me, but I ain't no bitch I ain't no fake motherfucka and no I don't switch, I don't roll over and turn over trying to get rich ain't no bitch in me ain't no fake in me just real trying my best out here staying hard then steal I'm too real to squil I'm to raw one hundred percent pure raw an uncut, tried of these fake motherfuckers out here faking snitching over a buck trying to take me out of the game when they roll around with that bass in the trunk hating me instead of the game when the rules and regulations are unspoken but simple and plain trying to take the life out of me while I'm just trying to maintain no rolling over bitch nigga I'm taking mine pay my bail lawyer fees and prepare to do my time waiting to get back on my get back so I get back to the life on the grind tried of these bitch made niggas out here wasting my time. Time to get back so I get back to the life shine sticking to the game plan like the world was mine haters throwing salt in the game hating on me everytime I hit the grind raw and uncut sticking to the code don't snitch don't squil and get it sold sticking to the game plan that always untold changing up the game I never get old, ain't no bitch in me I'm out here sticking to the game plan loaded up and ready to fight for my life stuck in the game sitting on white raw one hundred percent pure only the real can come and pick up the cure in a world unspoken no turning over on these neighborhood soliders just stick to the code do the crime and do the time plede the fifth and keep the story untold and don't fold don't take the next man down keep your head up and eyes open and watch the money come round sticking to the rules and regulation don't hate its to late in the game for that do the crime do the time the time and prepare to get back on your get back keep your mouth closed plede the fifth and your playa potna will keep you out with the cost but if you turn bitch and snitch then its your lose it costs to be the boss in these mean streets out here its costs to get sticking to the rules and regulations to keep it moving on these streets staying one hundred percent pure if you get caught up my nigga you know your, potnas have the cure staying raw and uncut living the life of shine staying on the grind if you snitch on me potna your no potna of mine, they can't take the life for me never snitch I'm no bitch one hundred percent pure homie if you get caught and holla at the cure sticking to the game plan one hundred percent pure.

PIED PIPPER

I gotta stay hot weather I'm on or not I'm blazing hot you can feel me coming when I'm blazing up the block, I'm the pied pipper here to take all you got once I'm on I can't stop here to keep the game on lock, holding the lock and key I know these other motherfuckers ain't as real as me. I'm the pied pipper you paying me because you suppose to be like the bull when I'm hot red is all I see hot to the touch nigga, ain't a nigga out here cold as me mesmerizing the block like I'm suppose to, you not just following my tune I touched yo ear and chose you I'm hot so turn it up a lot because I told you, you suppose to catch the ears to the street when you put in time, they owe you I'm stay hot you should throw away that other fake shit they sold you, you can all follow me ain't a nigga alive out here that I can see hot to the touch cold as me, ain't no quincemence me and you was meant to be, they tried to get off scots free. I had to burn up the block its time to come out of pocket and pay me, if not I'm taking all them with me all I had to do was find the key now me and this tune came together I can feel again the beat chose me, me and you were meant to be, you can see the heat rising off my back I'm too hot to forget me, that mesmerizing you hear in yo hear is me, I'm hot because I'm suppose to be, we can all be free, yest turn up the volume keep yo ears open and follow me. I chose you and this beat chose me, ain't a nigga alive out here hot like me, even if you bite me you could never be like me mesmerized by the drumline this beat excites me together we hold the lock and key, since they forgot to pay me I'm taking them all with me, now I'm part of the beat so now the beat is me, all I gotta do to open the door is put the lock to key, I stay hot don't you see the trail of fire the follows me. I came back lined with the track to make sure they hear me I can never be sorry sincerely now they all follow me, instead of with me you against me, I guess you didn't notice the raging fire that lies inside of me, ain't a nigga alive that can burn up the block like me, how do you like the taste of your own medicine, as I touch yo town and make everthing around crumble to the ground with me plus the surround sound putting another nail in the coffin ever time you hear the bass pound. I'm here to take what you owe I'm the hottest thing around I'm trying to figure out how you didn't know, you must pay what you owe, rain sleat hail snow, you didn't pay up so now we all gotta go how didn't you know. This song is over with I'm done with stereo, now I got what I wanted its time to go. I'm hot I'm the pied pipper here to take all you got once I'm on I can't stop, here to keep the game on lock

I can't stop!
I'm too hot
I can't stop.

EARLY SUNDAY MORNINGS

I remember when the Koolaid didn't last so long, waking up to the smell of bacon, early Sunday morning yawning, momma making us a hot plate making sure she made enough, just incase you woke up late, she made the food, but you had to make your own plate, she made Sunday mornings you could appreciate, hommery grits, and pancakes, fried eggs, and fresh made, homemade iron skelet waffles and crispy bacon to go around, you know how momma got down always had the table smelling good if anybody could put us back together you know she could blurry eyes and open plates always willing and able, listening to the laughter echo around the kitchen table, back in the day there was never love missing around the kitchen helping momma around the kitchen early morning asking for her early morning sugar, her price for cooking us a hot plate, I know you can relate. I love the smell of breakfast in the morning. Family life is my bacon and eggs, momma only had one job to keep five mouths feed and a roof over head, keeping us from fighting to reduce bloodshed, I was the neighborhood fat kid around the block so you know we stay feed. My momma is my cinnamon and spice of life, thanks for breakfast momma, always ready to pay the price and I never think twice, to me my momma made life, she's the only one who could calm me down and talk to me, a little momma's boy. If you saw my momma then I know you saw me, just as shy as can be. My momma made life for me, always there to help me polish up my ego, if I had something to hide inside, she knew how to let me, let it go, unless it was a homemade waffle then let go my ego. Momma made me love the life that family brings, waking up to the sounds of early Sunday morning music, the sunshine hurting my eyes. I was her little man, but I always felt like a king listening to momma fry eggs, listening to her and the radio sing. So many wonderful memories my childhood and Sunday mornings brings, sometimes I look back and wish I could go back through time just one more time, just to sit at the table and soak in some Sunday morning sunshine, with a dash of sugar from yo little bugger. Sometimes I wish I could go back and never come ??? remembering the smiles and faces of the past that passed on, thinking about ??? time has pass and so many lives that passed on, remembering the taste of ??? our hot meals where gone. It's a shame sometimes that life has to ??? remembering the flavor after the meal is gone, dame life goes on, hoping you appreciate if you were a friend of the family then you always had a hot plate, now I'm just left with stories and memories of the pass, holding on to em tight, hoping they last, remembering Sunday morning momma and family that I miss, momma could could your whole world with just one kiss, thinking about the family, life I miss, memories come in handy when you feel alone like this. Keep a hot plate for me in case I'm running late, or even if its a plate I might miss and next time you see me hold on tight, this might be the last time I see family, life and life just might pass on thinking of the days when Kool aid didn't last so long. Remembering momma singing me a love song forever holding on to life and my memories until my life goes on, just remember the next time you see me might me the last time so hold on tight. I gotta go now momma I gotta catch the late flight. I love you momma goodbye goodnight.

FALLING

Falling through space and time, feeling the weight of the world and the pressure of everyday life constantly trying to bring me down I feel like I can't see the ground, there no end in sight, there no end to the frustration only dark no light, fatigued by the pressure that life brings, hunted by father time, and the seconds that follow, falling through space through time holding on to the timeline of life, wondering how my life started to drift away, there's no gleamer of light in sight, only space no light, there's nothing real to hold on to, only space, and time, and the weight of the world that hunts me. Seconds turn into minutes, minutes turn into hours, making hours feel like centuries, it's been so long I forgot I was fallin' the only thing I have left our my past memories, of a time left behind, holding onto my memories that give me chance to finally face this face of mine, with no light in sight, I can't figure out which way is down, falling through space, through time listening the sounds of death echo, up or down now it doesn't matter to me, I'm falling in love again with my precious memories. These sweet memories of mine of a time that once was when I use to receive love from above, falling through space, through time searching for a familiar face in a familiar place, searching for something real to hold on to, a place to visit and roam through, thoughts take me away to a place from yesterday as I continue to fall through time and space and drift away, and for a second I feel at home, even though I'm surrounded by darkness all alone in a place all it's own, falling through space, through time wondering where did the time go, I don't know, hiding somewhere between the lines somewhere in space and time searching for light, wading through this dark life of mine, stuck in the past remembering this life of mine, falling through space, through time holding on to the timeline. I'm gone and forgotten, lost in space trapped by time.

Falling further away from life, or has life already ended and I'm just trapped in the minds of others, who can forget a light like mine, I'm so alone in my drift downward with no life in sight. I've been falling for so long, I forgot what life is like without my light. There's so much darkness around me as DEATH surrounds me, here falling through space, through time, listening to the echos of this voice of mine, this has to be more then just a dream, but yet less then reality, searching through my memories, falling through space with <u>time</u> and <u>me</u>, trying to catch a brief vision of life's landscape, a most not yet forgotten, a picture to picture of something loved and lost through time but never forgotten, a loved one, a favorite place. Something real to hold on to as I continue to fall with the weight of the world on top of me, on my desent through, space through time with a light I can't see I wonder if time will wait for me, trying to hold on to the timeline and the life that once was mine, searching for happiness, a loving hug, a friendly handshake or an intimate moment spent with a loved one someone close to the heart, life gone but not forgotten, left with memories of the heart. I don't know where to start. Falling through space, through time holding on to the timeline forever missing this life of mine, counting the seconds watching the minutes pass, searching for something to hold on to, as I continue to search my past that passed on, with the weight of the world on my shoulders and life behind me, if I ever slip away from your mind, you'll know exactly where to find me. Falling through space and time holding on to the timeline, searching through my memories remembering this life of mine. I'm just a memory away I'm never hard to find.

R I P
E N E
S A

BACK N DA DAY

Remember back in the day doing flips over fences, just another street soldier living the life in the trenches, back in the day when pussy wasn't new to me, a little hard headed youngsta wasn't nothing you could say or do to me, little knuckle head trying to be as hard as I could be, living in a world where momma ruled over me back talking as I walked away, when she asked me what I said, I said nothing and walked away, back in the day when the streets had love for me, before the grind took its toll on me, sorry momma I got eat money got a hold on me. Hitting the block, match ten for ten, remembering when I use to pump gas for change moms had my life on lock. So side jobs was an everyday thang, an up coming youngsta on the block waiting to grow up just to let my nuts hang. I saw money making, and made it an everyday thang. Saving up to hit DA Block and let the chrome feet swang, remembering back in the day I was never alone, you can call me at home staying up all night saying nothing on the phone, kickin it with the neighborhood big booty cutie I done seen before. I could call her any time and get her alone so I could get some more, back in the day as a youngsta what <u>more</u> could you ask <u>for</u>. Back in the day when family and friendship was the strongest smoking blunt after blunt to see who could stay up the longest, back in the day when the bond was strongest. When everyday felt like it would last forever we always stayed tight like birds of a feather no matter the weather we were always down for whatever. Soaking up the sounds on the radio, the could never let me go, holding on to family until family let me go, coming from the town where 2 short was a hero, helping to put the town on the map listen to I got five on it, you need fade I stay straped, listening to the sounds of life a little nickle and dime ass nigga afraid to roll the dice. I hate to loose. I had too much to gain and everything to loose, young and full of cum with everything to prove, just another day in the life I live with everything to loose, back in the day when I was young, I'm not a kid anymore but I sitback and wish I was a kid again, back in the day when it was more kitchen cuts then braids more condoms then AK's, momma made sure we had a refrigerator stock so we could eat for days, back in the day when I use to help her deseed her weed box she loved my hard headed ass she never kept the box locked, playing around with mommas rusty pistal with no bullets to cock, back in the day before probation way before they started hating, remembering before the sell cocane but after the first time I had a strap aimed at the brain, but in the day when I was almost too much to handle and too cold to fuck with, one chance to cross the line and yo ass was done with back in the day a mean mug was all you'd get a little hard headed motherfucka who didn't want to be fucked with rolling around the block with the dogs I run with back in the day fading up for the next blunt to hit, back in the day when you couldn't tell me shit, growing into a man going through the things that men deal with I done seen it all these niggas can't tell me shit, remembering back in the day when I was young, I'm not a kid anymore, but I often sitback and remains and wish I was a kid again. Dame I wish I was a kid again. I wish I was a kid again.

*Radio Hitting

CRACK LIKE THIS

Putting me all together, making sure all the pieces fit together bag me up tie me off like new age crack getting ready to sale to the street I'm burning up the block now I remember when ramen noodles was all I used to eat, but now I'm back to the street making more then mince meat Mr. Connect DA Block putting everything together to make ends meet, how you loving yo boy like the first time really standing on his feet, poking and proding making sure I'm as real as can <u>be</u> once all the pieces are put together then you'll see, it ain't another one like me once I hit DA Block so everyone can get a piece of me, be careful I'm hot to the touch I bet you didn't think I'd come together and burn up DA Block so much. Don't close yo ears I'm too much, sitting heavy walking down yo block and every step making yo block cra cra crack like this, in yo area tearing ya apart I bet you ain't seen it come together and burn up the block like this making yo head cra cra crack like this, once you hit DA Block don't miss, in this game of fame its easy to fall apart like this but I ma ma make it crack like this gangsterish with a gansta twist I hit and don't miss open up yo ears and listen to the beat like this, ma ma make it crack like this, a little out of the ordinary put me back together again a little something more the extraordinary stepping out the belly of the beast with my palms hairy, they told me to write this single because my life was scary, pulling at me at all ends trying to rip me up and tare me, but I could never be a ZERO if you listen to yo block. They tell you I was the pushing mens HERO if you press tare we'll take you back to ZERO, we all fall apart but now I'm all together again, I'm so hot I'm changing the weather again, don't you see me floating in the wind, putting together the machine that was born to win, we're out here to take over DA Block and keep your dial on lock so count me in ma ma make it crack like this keeping it gangsterish with a lemon lime twist I bet you ain't never felt the BASS like this. I'm a little something extraordinary out of the ordinary I hit and don't miss, tearing up yo radio stations when you hear the beat hit like this ??? I'm gangsterish mix in with some of that and a lot of this putting the pieces of the puzzle together now I clockwork like this ma ma make it crack like this I'm super not superficial I hit DA Block like this they wind me up let me go and let me hit like this, when you put the piece of the puzzle together like this you can't miss now listen to the BEAT kick like this ???

Gangsterish with a gangstas twist. I bet they ain't bring it together and ma ma make it crack like this. I hit and don't miss. You open up your ear holes and turn it up like this. This is that shhh don't tell em what we are we're something extraordinary something like star putting together the right piece so I go far, with the right pieces you can't miss because we ma ma make it crack like this ma ma make it crack this, we ma ma make it crack like this, we ma ma make crack like this.

I'M HERE

You asked for help and I'm here, the picture is always there even if it's not yet clear, I'm there to help you, catch you when you fall, when your back is against the wall, the one to lift you up to help you stand tall. I'm the one here to listen to you every time you call the one to give you a helping hand to make sure you can't fall. I'm the one that stood by your side and watched you go through it all. I'm the one that can't fall. I stand too tall, if your path ever gets blocked I'm the one you call, older then the sands of time brighter then the light of the sun, if your wishes are at all possible, then they shall be done, to me you are the chosen one picked by the one known by all, remember I'm the one that stands to tall to fall. You can find a piece of me everywhere, and a piece of me in everyone, they may call you names, but to me you remain my son thy will be done, remember the remains the chosen one, I'm here to listen and help until the job is done, cool you off in the hottest summer sun, they may throw stones at your glass house but remember you remain the chosen one, make your light shine bright, brighter then the brightest son, let thy will be done until thy job is done. I'm here to warm you up in the coldest of winters, here to guide you with light in the darkest night even on earth I can give you flight, the chosen one. You remain the one and only one until thy will is done. I'm here to guide you home when your heart sings to me, if your blood is spelt then let it be, now you see what is. Is meant to be. I am everywhere its never hard to find me. I stand tall watching you go through it all, here to give you a hand before you start to fall, I'm here watching even if you can't tell, here watching you sleep breathing every inhale. You may not see me when you wake up, but I will always leave a piece of me with you, you don't think I don't hear but I do I left freewill up to you the journey is up to you. I'll be here to hold you up in your time of need, watching things grow, growing a tree remembering the seed, set strongly and firmly in place. I'm here to help comfort you while time takes its place, but remember everything that starts has to end. I will remain with you from beginning to end, speaking in your ear like the blowing of the wind, remember the road is up to you. I can set the course but the journey is up to you. Sometimes it feels like I don't listen to you but I'm here to let you know I do. I sprouted the seed I could never forget about you, let thy will be true, the journey is always up to you, I'll be at the end patiently waiting for you, I've set the course now the rest is up to you, until then I'm here waiting for

Y O U.

GAME

Never let these haters know where you stay. Never let these motherfuckers know what game you play. Make sure you keep business to yo self, never let em know the price you pay. In this game make sure you always protect where you lay you never know when you might have to cockback and spray no mercy my nigga. Niggas die everyday my nigga life ain't fair this is the game we play, always watch yo back these hunger niggas see you eating and don't know how to act quick to take the short cut and pull a kick door and take yo whole stack. Never sleep with the enemy, no friends in this industry, my enemyes, enemy is no friend to me, they could be the same niggas out there trying to kill me. Sometimes the closest nigga to you is the one to do you in, quick to stab a nigga in the back a leave the knife in. Friends turn to foes all over the dough, never think twice about kicking these backstabbers to the curb rain, sleat, hail, snow, you never know even the closest nigga to ya, will try to do ya over the snow, hating ya life and the price of blow even if they got it for the low, you never know like Johnny Depth in Blow, niggas quick to snitch in this game of snow you never know make sure you keep yo dirt on the low, like Robert Deniero in Heat watch the way the game goes, ears open and eyes on the prize these niggas love to hate and they often tell lies, out here in these street your best friend could be the devil in disguise, keep yo eyes on yo backside clip loaded and ready when it's time to ride, never letting bullshit slide niggas kidnap for show get rid of bodies on the low you can't show love to these niggas who lust for dough remember I told you so. Jealousy will get you killed, these bitches don't give a fuck, these bitches a set a nigga up to after you fuck the bitch she might turn around and fuck you. Gold-digging ass bitch quick to spread wide to get rich. Money over a bitch fuck pussy she can have her shit, these bitches should already know pussy is the price for dick. I'll call a bitch when I my dick get thick, using their pussy to pay rent, turn yo back on the ho and she'll sneak out and take yo shit, make that bitch open up wide and get all you can get, from me dick is all <u>your</u> <u>going</u> get, ole good for nothing ass bitch, trying to use her pussy to get rich. Never sleep with these haters around they'll get you for what you got a forget what they saw when it all goes down, you know how niggas get down, rob a nigga blind without making a sound, and still come around, it might be the same nigga you grew up with, the same nigga you represent and threw up with you know how shady niggas get, these money hungry niggas don't play around, as long as they come up, who cares who falls down, loving the smell of the next niggas money when it all goes down. Never let em know where you keep yo stash at, yo garunteed ass at, these niggas a bleed you dry and take all yo assets. Quick to cockback and make a nigga lay where you stay niggas die everyday, give me the money fuck the nigga that died today. Smiling faces tell lies and I found proof, found my stacks missing, and that nigga riding in my brand new coupe, nigga come swoop, tried to throw a nigga for a loop, dame the nigga got me it's only one thing I can do, sitting here ready to ride waiting for my nigga to slide through, I almost forgot these niggas golddigg too. Play the game smart and always watch the nigga closet to you, always remember these niggas don't give a fuck about you, keep yo eyes open and these niggas out ya pocket, never let em in once the start they won't stop it.

WHISPERS

Whispers awaken me from sleep, voices I can't see taunt me, taken time away from sleep, taring at my mental state, these voices don't know me, something wrong, unsure of the area of pain that needs to be released from me, haunted by voices that have awaken me, trying to take me away from sanity, continuously taunting me, driving this sane man insane I'm sick of the madness that needs to be cut away from my brain, searching for the insane parts as I start to pick through my brain, starting the pain watching the red rain, as I start to search through with persition, watching the red rain as the pain continues to blur my vision, taunted by voices I can't see, but I can hear with the clearest clearity, it has to be a way to deafen the voices that constantly continue to bother me, haunt me eating me alive inside this voices are driving me up the wall. I can't help it I must get rid of the pain that lie within my brain, cutting away at the madness watching the red rain fall, fighting the whispers that have awakened me fighting these inner demons that lie inside, where has this madness taken me, is this the madness that is making me mad, maybe the voices that haunt me are voices I never had, forgetting if its the voices or red rain driving me insane, feeling the warmth and the pain of the red rain that stains my face, this is the truest form of pain, trying to find the problems of life that lie within my brain. It was the whispers that have awakened me, so close and yet so distant I feel so far away from home watching the rain roam without my mirror I feel so alone, cutting at the madness that lies inside, insanity that torments me as I watch the red rain fall, while I search through the brain trying to find the source of pain that tries to hide inside releasing endorfins watching my body twich I wonder why I feel like this as I feel the rush of pain enter my body and travel up my spine constantly searching for this insanity of mine that lies deep in mind its so hard to find, but even I know every search takes time, trying my best to defeaten the whispers that haunt me. I'm trying to turn down the volume of whispers that taunt me, I can trust the pain watching the red rain fall, this pain is read but these voices of insanity are putting too much pressure on my brain mesmerize by the pain. Trying to remain calm through every rush and jolt of pain. I trying to figure out what part of sanity turned this sane man insane, poaking and proding at my brain that has been accompanied by red rain, the rain that never stops. I stop and for a moment to remember when life had a purpose numb from the pain holding a flap of skin trying my best to stay focused, living with the pain I'm going through its kind of hard to hold this flap of skin looking in the mirror as I again start to focus in trying to cut away the pain that causes havic to my brain, its easier to live with this physical pain then the stress and strain of this insanity that rotts my brain, searching to find a piece of mind and the madness that's eating me alive. Cutting away layer after layer of matter hoping I'm cutting the line just fine. Picking this brain of mine and I can't seem to stop the pain I can hear the voices in the back of my mind no matter how far I dig they continue to defeat me. Can somebody how can whispers I can't see continue to beat me, these voices are eating me alive, cutting away the madness I think I'm doing fine. Trying to cut away this pain of mine the voices are hard to get rid of. I can live with the pain, but I can't live with the strain that rotts my brain, trying to cut this madness out of my brain, the whispers that hide deep inside and rid myself of this grief and torment the pain inside trying to cut away the madness that tries to hide, hoping to ease the pain as I watch the rain fall, watching the lights dim as I start to loose focus, cutting away the madness that lies inside, looking for these voice that can't hide. The whispers start to deafen and the voices start to drift away. I cut deep enough to deafen the whispers but now the red rain won't go away, feeling the light go dark looking at my reflection of two shades, wondering where have I gone, there's nothing but insanity now, the sane man's gonna, the lights continue to dim as I watch the rains fall, trying to fight the whispers that put an end to it all. I put an end to the whispers and the whispers put an end to it all, light off the rain stops and that all no more whispers no more voices no more stain and no more pain at all.

KISS OF DEATH

These niggas keep fucking with death I wonder why they long to die, longing for the Kiss of Death and the long Kiss Goodbye. I wonder what it is about me they all despies, trying to keep a lid on me praying and praying for my demise, I'm straped up, out numbered and out gun this hard life got me on the run out here fund raising chasing the raising sun, it's either hell or jail out here living with bail, fuck these nigga I'd rather take jail then hell climbing up the ladder reinventing the sale of soft, I can't stop until I get off so bitch nigga get off me, moving my chess pieces before these niggas off me. So long and goodbye busting when I see that hate in yo eye, they can't make me slip but Lord you know they try, go hard or go home out here with my bandana across the face, 9 times out 10 they won't remember my face when I face to face with the nigga trying to take my place. It's fuck these niggas out here born to hate. I'm starving out here nigga I'd be damed if I let these niggas steal my plate, hungry and just ate making my move before its way too late, always ready to stand and deliver and hit you from yo head to yo liver fuck these niggas I got pain to deliver, chrome tight you know I'm coming for that ass you seen the end of my barrel spit white light, explosive like dynamite killing these niggas excites me, these niggas love to hate me because they don't play the game like me, they bite me because they really want to be like me, now these niggas bought more guns to make sure they out number me. The next move is plain to see, but remember my nigga ain't no bitch in me. I wait for the day when steal is all you see, these nigga don't even know they long to die and I don't know why, I feel like Pac, I'm real and real niggas can't die, even when I'm gone they will never forget me. But I bet a million to one they won't remember the nigga that million doller hit me. Most likely these niggas won't survive the night, their mesmerized by my guns white light, my nigga just walk this way. I could give a fuck about you, niggas like you die everyday from guns and gun spray, these pussy ass niggas make my dick hard and nothing excites me more then hitting these niggas up two times harder then hardcore with this lyrical war, putting slugs in these niggas mean mugs making these niggas uglier then before keeping these niggas in check in times of war, if you long to die then what they fuck you still alive sugar coatin no more, die motherfucka die like I said before, this niggas been dead before brought this zombie nigga back to life just to even the score him said him want war, but him don't know that fucking with him will make your brain soar, just like them birds that fly down south I wonder what this nigga will do after I blow his brains out, fuck a knock out. I'm here to put yo life out, ask them niggas in yo background they'll show you what I'm talking about, I'm a real nigga with much clout, like Master P I'm bouty bouty what would yo brain do without me, you'd be in the red to doubt me, all this nigga got was a full clip. I'm the nigga that made the game flip, sipping and dipping in yo pockets hitting these niggas harder then hardcore always prepared for war, die motherfucka die like I said before I'm real 100% pure I could have swore I killed this nigga once before, I seen his face somewhere before, fuck the battle my niggas I'm here to win the war. What is it about me you despise they pray and pray for my downfall and pray for my demise

I know these niggas hate me, I can see the hate in their eyes yo death ain't no surprise to me. I had to hit em one more time, he still looked alive to me, face to face with my number one all to earse yo face, death call bitch nigga now take yo place. Bandana around my face just incase they remember my face sometimes you only need one gun to put these bitch niggas in place now take yo place.

SUCH A BEAUTIFUL THING

Such a beautiful way die holding gunmetal listening to bullets fly. What a wonderful way to die, watching the clip get rid of that everlasting twinkle in yo eye, such a beautiful way to die hollering at the triggerman to kiss your brain goodbye it's such a beautiful way to die griping the gunmetal now kiss that ass goodbye.

I'm only skin blood flesh and bone here to put your flesh to chrome don't trip take a clip to the dome as soon as I turn the heat on, when it's on it's on I can't go without ya die alone, they ready to cremate ya I don't even know if yo maker will take ya, with yo face half gone, when its time to get down with the get down I get down with the chrome, million doller hit on my own, when you lay down, you stay down ain't no more running home, don't be surprized you should feel lucky to die out here to rub out that well known twinkle in yo eye. (Die bitch Die). Death is real and bullets kill real niggas too. I'm a real nigga expecting the nigga to do what real niggas do, give me something to blow through, you ain't nothing but skin and tissue to me. If you can't handle these niggas, my nigga send them niggas to me, I'm run with the A.C.T. with my strap beside me, ain't nobody gone know ain't no need to find me, then niggas ain't no flesh of mine as long as them niggas marked for death I think I'll doing just fine, making these niggas walk the plank everybody knows bullshit stank, they said forget the beef I ate, and I can't, killing these niggas feels so good, putting my chrome to yo dome just to make it understood, it's me and you nigga plus my triggerman. They don't understand how killing these niggas feel so good, with all respect to the hood. Killing this niggas ever so slightly, (STOP), my nigga if I could I would fuck these niggas for cutting me down because of how high I stood, I forever rep my hood I wouldn't stop even if I could I can't stop, I can't stop until these niggas breathing in wood, breathing in wood I like the sound of that. I know my life will be alot better when I put these niggas head of flat, I'm trying to make yo head bounce back when I attack with the Gat with some of this and some of that, yeah I love the sound of that, setting the infa red on yo head just to let yo know where I'm at, putting yo flesh to chrome, now all yo mighty men are all gone, and they all died alone. I told these niggas when it's on it's on, handling my issue with my military issue, blowing through your tissue, I could give a fuck if yo family missed you. I can't miss you, so goodbye and so long, these backstabing ass niggas been alive for too long, once your gone, your gone and you can't come back, hollowing yo flesh and bone with ever twist from the Gat, nigga that bullshit stanks and I can't leave my chrome alone got me blowed stuck in the zone making sure these niggas all die alone. Release the beast and watch yo lights dim, hit him him him then him, yo chances of survival are slim, (you trying to tell that's the nigga that got buried today was him and him), I don't know shit, there's Mr. Trigger Man what don't you ask him, ashes to ash dust to dust them niggas tried to hit me so I had to bust. Never believe the word of a man you can't trust, flesh to chrome I tried to hold back the lust but I had to bust ashes to ashes now niggas dust to dust them niggas tried to hit me so I had to bust.

CAN'T GIVE UP

Can't never give up hope, it's all apart of the game. You gotta roll with the punches pick up yo face and move on and maintain, strive to stay alive weather its with a nine or a nine to five, you can't let the ups and downs get ya, when it's all said and done you'll be standing alone, with nobody standing with ya, so what if they put you down, and them fake niggas don't come around, that's the time when you suppose to pick up the pace and show em how you really get down, when it's all said and done you shouldn't have to regret yo outcome, let thy will be done until the job is done. You can't give up, you can't let go, don't give up yo life just because they said so, don't hold on to the bullshit, let that bullshit go. Life ain't fair and it never will be, I can't even remember the smell of all the bullshit life sent me, what will be will be. Kay Sara Sara, if you don't live yo life, then your life will live without ya, take advantage of every breath. Keep yo head up and let these haters doubt ya always do your best strive to stay alive. Leave them haters in the dust, and never ever ever fuck with a nigga you can't trust. I've been pushed around, kicked, stomped on and woke up one morning with my head on flat. I had to piece myself back together again. I thought I'd never come back from that, but I'm now back, to give this bullshit back, now I'm back on top again I'm here to make sure that I don't fall back. It's all apart of the game, if you give these haters a chance and they'll drive the sanest man insane, bullshit is apart of the game, fuck em all then do your best to stay up and maintain I do they same thang, then catch em with their mouths wide open and let yo nuts hang, run up if you want to, we can chete chetie bang bang dealing with these hating ass motherfuckers tome is an everyday thang, just hold on and stay strong, and just do the dame thing you can't give up, you gotta roll with the punches dust yourself off and keep it rolling. Stick to the game plan them niggas ain't knowing, always keep yo head to the sky no matter which way you going, these niggas ain't knowing, it's just another day in the life, we all roll the dice paying the price to live life, and believe me life ain't nothing nice, it's not always peaches and cream like Pac said keep yo head up, and just step toward your dreams, collect that mean green separate the real from the fake and kick these fake niggas off the team before it's too late, it's all apart of the team, no matter what you going through it's somebody out there going through the same shit as you, just don't give up, keep yo head up and just do the dame thing, and no telling what this life will bring, remember even in the coldest of winters the sun still comes out to melt the snow, I tell these motherfuckas you reap what you sow just lean toward the direction you want your life to go, it's all a part of the game, do whatever you gotta to do out here to maintain while you do the dame thing, don't swallow your pride when your dying inside, tell em to open up wide don't let that bullshit slide, just keep it moving. I can garuntee you'll start to see your life improving, never ever fuck with a nigga you can't trust shake them fake niggas off they so sandlers, only you know what life got you going through, it don't matter what them niggas do, you gotta do you, keep yo head up and strive to stay alive no matter what you do, and remember these hating ass niggas are going to hate you for whatever you do, it's all apart of the game, you can't give up no matter what happen to you, you gotta keep your head up, and continue to do you, you can't give up, even when life gives up on you. The direction of your life always depends on you. You gotta dust these haters off to give you room to start a new, and don't give up the fight, you hold the key to control your life.

WHAT IS IT YOU DESPIES

What is it about me do you despies. I know you hate me I can see it burning in your eyes, and eyes don't lie, they tell the tail of unloyality and hate. I can see your just another starving motherfucka ready to take from my plate, calling out these motherfuckas who were born to hate, now what is it you hate about me remember you sparked the hate not me, I know its not the money or the fame or these bitches in the game, like scaface I'm one of the last of a dying breed most of these nigga live to dessive, but me I follow the rules and regulation to the game even with the world against me hurting, while I'm waiting for the hate to seize or the time. When its time to release the <u>beast</u>, sometimes all one can do is turn up the heat. I'm a hood nigga all I got is the street. I paved a path you can't beat, I brought the food to the table when it was time to eat. You suppose to keep your mouth shut when you get caught up, not throw up the right information, speaking it and leaking it all, they caught one domino to make us all fall. If you can't handle the heat then hand it to me, remember them niggas crossed the game not me, you know me riding from state to state like I'm suppose to be, don't worry about me your not suppose to see, if they saw me get down with the get down they'd propable slip up, bitch up, and let all the pieces fall, hating me for taking a piece from yall, I guess you can never ever trust a nigga you can't trust. You can never underestimate the next mans greed. Some of these niggas will cut down your tree before you can even water your seed. I know you hate me I can see it your eyes don't hate the playa hate the game, hate the bitches the money and the fame why blame me these ups and down are all apart of the game. Why would you point the finger at me, these motherfuckas got caught up and now they blame it all on me, they crossed the game not me and it's plain to see I'm free and you not that's really why you hate me. I can see the hate in your eyes. You don't have to tell me. I can see it's me you despies your hate for me is so strong I can see it seaping outside, what happen to money power respect, honor and loyalty, these snitches ass niggas can't do shit for me, I know we all know the rules and regulations to the game. They put me on the chess board and told me to play, even though they don't even play by the rules, their trying to play me for a fool, I can't make the wrong move. I can see the hate burning in their eyes, telling the tail of these snitches that lie, their trying to push me off the table like Kane and Able, what is it about me you despies. I know you hate me because your eyes don't lie. They got caught up snitched and lied, what is it about the truth are you trying to hide. I thought we weren't suppose to let the bullshit slide. It's time for me to let go I never will understand these niggas who don't play by the rules no <u>more</u>. If this nigga snitch on me, and that nigga snitch on him because that nigga got caught up and they all against him, what would that nigga do to you, probably the same thing because that nigga don't really give a fuck about you. Watch the playas in the game, these nigga who fiend for the bitches money and the fame, these niggas with no loyalty who don't belong in the game, snitching to them is an everyday thang, don't try to play me like a fool, nigga I know the game, hating just to hate me, mad because you ain't me, got caught up now all of a sudden they pointing their fingers at me, so I know you hate me. I can see it in your eyes, praying for my demise, always pay attention to the eyes because the eyes don't lie, no love nigga. Kiss that ass goodbye. I knew the nigga hate me and snitches don't lie, praying for my demises, I wonder if they think I'm a just let this bullshit slide, everything already out in the open, so I don't try to hide.

MY AK

Imagine being swept away by my AK, ziped up and carried away they may remember you from day to day, but most don't care niggas die everyday, I bet now they realize the clips don't play, so don't play with me I'm armed to the teeth seriously, sue fly sue don't bother me. I got this killa lock up, chain up inside of me. Awaiting release, you might want it with me, but you may not be able to handle the beast, ready to crease you up like some Sunday slacks you've been asking for the beef, and I'm telling you hear is where it's at. With a pull of the trigger, I stand to stand and deliver to put your face in the dirt. When your all dead this extra clip won't hurt. I'm from a place where the AK's spray, and for crossing the game you might have to pay, and life ain't cheap, without my AK to spray. I don't know what I'd do, sometimes I die on the inside when I'm cocked and aimed at you ain't nothing else to except pull the triggerman, that stands in my right hand, lock and load ready for whatever comes my way just another day in the life with my AK, picture a picture of life plus destruction, plus a man with an AK down for busting. What a sight to see, don't worry I'm just taking care of this beef that was brought to me. Most people don't know what lies in the pit, its worse then seeing one of your men get hit, nothing I could say could describe the sight, never giving up on life until they blow out the light. Surrounded by darkness darker then night, no time for stage fright. I might be found on the front page, this is the correct time to release the beast from the cage, sometime my AK is the only thing to destroy the rage that lies in the streets, you won't be able to find me unless you find my heat. I'm real from head to feet ready to feel yo box with you from head to feet, nine, Mossbergs Mac's and AK owe my, when as time to face the beast you can kiss that ass goodbye, don't bring your problems my way, no time for these hating ass niggas I'm in love with my AK, such a beautiful weapon always ready to fill a nigga up without question. When your facing the fire there is no second guessing. I'm sitting heavy tell me why would these niggas want to test me, nigga I ain't the one my semi automatic is built for the pit, lead from me is all you're gone get. I saw the hate in his eyes so I had to spit don't fuck with a nigga when his armed and lit. Another day in the life keeping them down in the pit, keeping the lights off living with my AK the opposite of soft. Fucking with me the pit is all you get. I saw the hate in his eyes so I had to spit. Now imagine being swept away zipped up and carried away while I'm toting my AK, they may remember you from day to day, but most of these niggas don't give a fuck, because niggas die everyday. Everyday I thank GOD for my AK living the life I live sometimes, your life is the price you pay my nigga. Niggass die everyday, keeping my AK by my side incase they try to make me pay, I don't know what else to say I'm just deeply in love with my AK I don't know what else to spray.

WHAT IF

What if I told you I've seen the world blow up a thousand time, talked to a man that give his life to a land mine, he told me death ain't hard to find, what if I said I've seen a meteor hit the ocean flood like it was said before, up all night ready for the 40 days and 40 nights of down pour, what if I told you I met a man that could end all war, he told me war is money son what do you think we're fighting for. What if I said I've seen a battle field with every life lost, every dream, every soul of man that life brought, bodies laying in the battle fields with open graves rotting inside because they've been missing for days, what if I told you life was death, but you can always find life in every breath what if I told you I saw a blind man see, he said I was marked for death because of the soul inside of me. What if I was the one who held your life in the palms my hands would you be the one to kill me because of the path, or would you be the one to trust me enough to ask me about the life you don't understand, watch me give your life back to you because I'm only a man, flesh and blood out to avoid the quicksand. What if I told you that dark wasn't hate but a shade of skin, apart of the big equation trying our best to win. What if I showed you a different part of life something you could hold on to, and take with you into the after life, what if after life, life was waiting for us. Ready to pick us back up again in heaven we trust. What if my semi-automatic weapon was for protection instead of an instrument to end life, what if my semi automatic weapon was a piece of paradise, what if there wasn't a place called death, just living life until life goes on left with immortal memerises after life passes on. What if I told you I seen a wise man jump off the mountain top and take flight not afraid to fall as he soared into the light, living on the wind thinking about nothing but life at the end of his desend what if I told you life was a lesson to be learn you have to watch where you stand your ground in life you can be burned, what if life was just a line for death releasing pain and torcher with every breath, how much life do I have left I keep a hold on life until the day I run out of breath, what is death, its just an end to life make sure when you let go you grab on to paradise. Is life just something we go through or is it something more about life, that life shows you, so please life show me the way. I've been waiting a long time to pass away. [I may drift away any day, running through life paying the price we pay. Sorry I can't stay they have a bullet with my name on it and their ready to spray, living life we all must pay holding onto life until I meet that day waiting for life to come and take me away.] what if I said you worship an instrument of death. What if I told you the reaper was the one to come and take your last breath what if I took you to the edge of the world and showed you the meaning of life. What if the answer you saw didn't look like paradise but instead you saw the beginning and end of life. What happens when the reaper come before its time, before the end of days, and before the end of ryme, the hand of the reaper is something you can't give back, what if I told you once your gone your gone, and you can't come back. What if I told you, you could find the answer to life in a tree, if you just listen to the tale of the tree grown from me would you be listening to the tree or a different side of me. I'm apart of life, so then life is me, just because I hold life in my hands doesn't mean GOD is me, I'm just trying to live life from the view I see. What if I told you life won't remember me spread my ashes to the earth letting me take the soul inside of me what if life and death was all it was suppose to be.

WHY AM I IN HELL

My GED wasn't good enough for me
So I got my masters on the street
No ten year anniversary for me
In the life of crime and everybody
Knows me living life with a class B
falonie tried to go to college but
finaceal aid had no love for me
trying to trap me for life for living
the life when I already paid the price
for living the hard life, trying to shake
these haters off my tail. I can't make
it in the real world the life of nine to
five, now I'm strapped up rolling with my
nine trying to find another piece and
piece of mine with no love except the
love I hold by my side trapped in, trying
to find a way out with my eyes open
hoping for a way to get out of hell
trapped by my own kind with love I
can't find trying to my piece before
they take what's mine. Soaking up the
game from the streets hoping they
can't find me, living the life on the
grind protecting me and mine pounding
the concreate under this hot sunshine
trying to shine, where these haters
try to take what's mine, ain't no love
in this life of crime, backstabbers
who don't do time plotting and scheming trying
to take what's mine, when grinding takes
time trying to reach the top before my
hearts stop ticking and I'm itching to let
go, living in these streets where it's blow
or push snow you ain't gotta tell me what
you want I already know. Trying to make
space before they try to take my place
living the life of crime and they already
knew my face, living with my nine by my
side protecting my space in this life of

grind she's any number one ace, living in
this world of no give just take
trying to fill up my plate before they
take it away, staying or grind
hustling under the hot sunshine
trying to shine living in a world
that's not mine. Stuck in hell
with nothing but time. Trying
to crawl out of this life
big time and of crime. I know it's something
better for me, something greater
for me, looking over my shoulder
ain't the life for me, no time
for me playing smart is
the only way for me climbing
to the top one way ticket
non-stop I can't stop I
ain't done yet I ain't
reached the top on a one
way mission to get it and
get gone. Living in the
world all on my own just
me myself and I sticking
to my chrome. Stacking
staying on the grind until
they call me home stuck
in the grind where the crime
is all it's own, hoping I
reach the top before they
call me home put down by
gun play with one to the
dome, until I'm dead and
gone hoping they miss me
when they call me home,
until then I'm stuck in
the grind trying to shine
like my chrome, stuck in
hell living a life of crime
trying to get out of hell
and reach the sunshine
protecting mine until they
come and take mine stuck
in the groose living a life that's

not mine. The life of grit and
grime living this life of big
time and crime pounding the street
under the hot sunshine.

Yous the yous the <u>bitch</u>
Who's the who's who is the <u>bitch</u>
Where's the where there's the <u>bitch</u>
Who's the who's yous the <u>bitch</u>
Over there his lips
Where's the where's there's the bitch
You now what happens when niggas
talk shit yous the yous you's the bitch
I got something for them niggas that
Shit

I know them niggas ain't talking to me
I ain't got time for bullshit running the
mouth as niggas. I can see the hate in
you face, don't fuck with me
bitch nigga stay in yo space
Don't be worring bout what I'm going
Bitch nigga I'm doing what I doing.
Drowning my drink don't be worried
about what I'm doing, bitch nigga I'm
doing what I'm doing. Stay in yo place
and don't invade my space, trying to
fuck up what I'm doing don't you see
me over here putting my drink in my
face, drunk as fuck ready to fuck
up face, so bitch nigga stay in yo place
I'm over here drowning my drink nigga
get out my face before I come over
there and slap the taste, don't bother
me nigga get the fuck out my face

Homie I'm in the kitchen cooking
chickens all day, bringing in that
lettuce and cheddar cheese so don't fuck
with these, cooking up everything ya
need to pla your mind at ease. Just
put the order in Homie got what you need

Homie I'll do you right and fulfill at your needs. Cooking in the kitchen to fulfill all your needs. Out slanging chicken like Rosscos waffels and chicken cooking up that good shit.

Fuck what you say I'm a stay high
Catch me flying with the birds
Staying sky high. Smoking and choaking
blunts all day everything I do, I do
the highway. Break it blunts down
and watch me roll up. They said it
illegal but It just don't give a fuck.
Doing what I wantta do bitch nigga
just because I wantta. Told me not
smoke, but bitch I gotta. To much
stress in the air bitch why do you
think I stay high watching the smoke
float in the air. Staying high till
I die, and I'm I high on life
told me to play the game, now bitch
its time for me to roll the dice.
paying the price and I got it for
the low. Hating on yo boy because
I used to push that snow. Why you
want to hate on me, trying to knock
my hustla bitch nigga you ain't no
kin to me, lighter in one hand
and a smoking blunt in the other, and
when I finish smoke this blunt its time
to smoke another. Staying sky high watch
the smoke fly, told you before I'm stay
high utill I die, your option doesn't
matter to me. If it was up to you
I'd be sober, broke and lonely. Bitch
nigga you don't own me. I'm my own
man nigga you can't tell me shit. You
too busy hating on me, and you don't even
know me. So bitch disown me. I'm a stay
sky high untill I die keeping a blunt to the sky
I'm trying to do good out here. I feel your hate
and now I know why. But fuck what you say I'm a
stay high anyone fuck what you say, bitch.

<u>Verbal ejection</u> the selection to end all wows sticking to the game plan and the high life I chose, with a tight group of friends and an eye on foes, just me being me living the life I chose. Staying sky high until my nigga high on life smoking in dough my nigga high on life living the high life getting high all night. No need to bite my tongue. I'm out here using my mouth piece, ears wide open sitting back ready for release. Grown manning it out here where we show no fear no need to bring it to the streets my nigga I'm already right here, living the high life with no time to show fear. I'm here to sit back relax smoke sac and fly sky high in the atmosphere, if there something to say then let it be known no time to fuck around I'm too busy drinking on patron trying to find a bad bitch so I can take home. No time for jealousy you can take your ass home I'm too busy getting lifted getting my drink on, but don't bite your tongue my nigga I can see the haste in your eyes with an itchy trigger finger, if you hate me then let it be known, if not get the fuck out my face and let me get my drink on don't you see me over me drinking gallons of patron. Dame I'm gone and I'm still on toes kicking with my potnas with an eye on foes. I can't help if your bitch is choosing you playing the game and you hating me because I'm not losing homie trust me you can have that bitch I'm kicking it with my potnas over here getting lit. So don't start no shit and waste my time hating me over some ass that's not mine, I'm chilling over there satisfying my own staying high as the sky with this bottle of patron. If you won't the bitch my nigga get gone I'm not worried about you nigga I'm over here stuck in the zone. If you want something with me I can send yo ass home but until then I'm over here relaxing downing my patron doing bother real niggas when you see them in them zone I'm not worried about you I'm just doing my own kicking back relaxing getting my drink on. Fuck that bitch nigga leave me alone.

POEM

This is my gun and no one esles this gun belongs to no one else but me, my gun doesn't exist without me my gun is dead in the hands of the enemy don't touch my gun my gun belongs to me to protect me when I'm face to face with the enemy that's what's to take my face and earse my space. This is my gun I keep it with me at all times always on my person and always in mind my gun is apart of me and never hard to find this is my gun a very good friend of mine. This is my gun used to protect never let your friend find the wrong hands and in up wet never forget your weapon remember your weapon is apart of you with an extra clip next to you cleaned and ready to produce gun spray hitting all targets from close range or far away. This is my gun that sleeps right beside me always an arm length away, cleaned, loaded armed and ready for action this is my gun my fatal attraction never afraid of action willing to do my biding and release reaction hitting the targets on point to meet my satisfaction release of chain reactions my weapons is always willing, cleaned cock loaded and ready to make killing. This my gun use to protect me don't give mercy we don't leave survivers and we don't lose. This is my gun my instrument of doom handy and ready to produce action. This is my gun my greatest satisfaction. This is my weapon for protection to use against my enemies loyal to me and only me this weapon belongs to no one else my gun is handled by me and only me when the dark surrounds I use my gun to see. This is my life my protection this is my gun that belongs to me. Such a beautiful piece of metal used to protect me, dead in the wrong hands and always on guard clean loaded and ready to protect waiting for the time when I'm ready. This is my gun and my gun belongs to only me to honor, respect, and to protect me. This is my gun the only weapon for me this is my gun the only one for me.

Trying to get me up for murder (murder)
Trying to get me up for murder (murder)
Planted evidence and leaked my name
To set me up and got the police my name
Trying to set me up for a murder. They're
Trying to set me up for a murder.
Crossed the line and blame it all on me
planted the evidence and called the
police on me, evidence planted and now
its them against me. They're trying to set
me up for a murder, trying to set me up for
a murder, (murder)

Planted the evidence in my place, fingerprints
and bloody shoes, setting me up to lose
Placing me at the scene of the crime, trying
to set me up for a crime that's not mine.
Couldn't use their vehicle so they stole
mine. Trying to set me up for a murder (murder),
trying to set me up for a murder. Trying to

catch me slipping and take what's mine, trying
to set me up for a crime that's not mine
planted the evidence and leaked my name
called the police and gave them my name
so they'll do the dirty work and split my frame
pointing the finger in my direction blaming me
for the blood the see blaming me for a murder I
didn't comment and now it's them against me
Trying to set me up for a murder (murder)
They're trying to set me up for a murder

Crossed the line and they're trying to blame it
on me blaming me for a crime I didn't comment
So they're all against me, evidence planted and
now it's them against me, somebody leaked my name
evidence planted and the choose me to blame

Go head cock back and pull it and put a bullet in my head. I ain't go shit to live for I'm already dead nothing to look forward to so I continue to take blunts to the head, I ain't running from shit I'm already dead so go head cock back and let go I'm waiting on you taking my last puff of the indo send me home to my maker so I can tell him what I'm in for I ain't running from shit. I already know what this shit for I seen you creaping through the shadows I seen you sneaking in the window. Caught me sleeping it shit I can do so go head cock back and aim I know when my life through so put your finger on the trigger my nigga and do what you do I been here waiting on you to do what you do I know the doors will open for me once my life is through only one life to live no time to renew I been sitting here potna waiting on you no time to waste so put your finger on the trigger and do what you do I can't take back sit I know when my life is through sitting here finishing my blunt in here waiting on you. Putting the blunt to the flame knowing my life is through. I guess my past caught up with me a hard life of dealing with the feeling of somebody watching me I guess this blunt is the end for me hammer cocked back with the barrel pointed at me facing more then a bullet I'm facing a full clip caught me slipping high as fuck. I can feel my eyes drip, no time to waste I ain't got much time left maintaining composure high as fuck my blunt's running out of breath can't back down I got to much pride for that cool calm and collective knowing the hammers cocked back left with blunt my pride my dick and my nut sack caught me slipping out here naked so I can't bust back how do you love that waiting for a bullet and I can't throw back if I wasn't sleeping then I could bust that. Go ahead and pull it I ain't got shit to live for I'm already dead maintaining my metal taking a blunt to the head ready to catch lead I ain't got shit to live for I'm already dead, watching the smoke surround my head facing more then a bullet I'm facing a full clip. I knew the game better then that I knew I shouldn't of slipped. Sit back and closed my eyes waiting for my head to flip. Take another puff and I'm gone one man gone took yo ass long enough to send my ass home another life lost from the first hand chrome.

Loving to see yo boy lose want me to turn out to nothing hating on yo boy trying to make something out of nothing hiding the real only showing the fake I want it all not just a piece of the cake staying in the struggle I can't lose dying to win no matter which road I choose I refuse to lose all these haters can stay fake while I rise to the top watching you pick up your face I gotta stay on the grind on a mission to get mine the hard life to the life of shine I'm getting what's mine you can love me or hate me homeboy you don't make me you need more then a salt shaken to shake me more then a dope case and probation to break me I'm on a money making mission I rather bet my cheese make me bet my weed bake me staying high through it all stacking up my chips collecting dollars so I sit tall built for it all living the life of a self made hustla with no time to waste no time for these haters so it's best the same face I'm counting money saving mine to take to the face only kicking it with the real if your fake I can't relate stuck in the struggle mind over muscle and I'm a money making mission on a mission for top dollars a life of top class high class models to pop bottles for me living the high life is the only life for me until the end of me when I done smoke a blunt for me I'm taking my money with me I can lose I'm dying to win staying strong with a tight grip watching the smoke blow in the air I too real with no time to pretend love counting my money sometime I forget what I spend spending chump change only stacking the nest keep my bond money ready just incase they try to arrest just another day just another one of life's test I can't lose I gotta stand tall and made through it all stroking to the game plan so I can't fall if I get caught up I got the cure wanting for me standing on my money making mission until the end of me. If I get caught I'll do the time for the crime because homie it ain't the end for me the killas and dope dealers on the black family almost kin to me when I die it ain't the end for me stuck in the struggle living life crused by the block with no chesee but to live the hard life just another one of life's test constantly counting my blessing and my dollars to remind myself that I'm blessed living this hard life with no time to second guess.

CASH FIRST

Cash first living the life, another day another price, just another day in the life. Hustling making that money roll in rolling the dice living the hard life pushing their ice don't you see me shining pushing this hard shit living this hard life caught between a rock and a hard place. Cash first homie chrome cocked protected my space I know da real can relate I'm trying to fill up my plate shaking these fake niggas off me living the hard life no time for softies living the hard life hustling pushing soft D I ain't no softy so fake nigga get off me. Cash first ain't no fronting out here ain't no stealing ain't no bitching ain't no snitching out here. Kicking with the real pros and con killers and dope dealers out here buying the block grinding hustling making money non-stop living the hard life rolling the dice out here living this hard life. No time for the cake out here, piece cooking cake. Keeping the money moving so get gone and buy a piece of your own, while I'm gripping the chrome taking blunts to the dome. I gotta have that cash first homie if you want to step into the zone I went out to get it and brought it back on my own I can push it bye myself I grind my own cash first homie if you want to step into the zone just another day in the life paying the price to live this hard life to me pushing Gs to OZs bring in pounds boats and quarter keys, no time for the fake, out here we push soft D, just another day living the life of a hustla like me. When fake bitches and dry snitches get no love from me fuck what you say just bring me the money, ain't shit funny out here living this hard life stuck in the grove just living my life, hustling trying my best just to maintain keeping my head up trying to keep my brain, from getting slain. Living this hard life trying to maintain. Nothing in life for free so cash first homie and don't come back unless you want pick up another sac from me but untill remember to holla back. Cash first nigga stay off my nut sac.

POEM

THESE PEOPLE

These people, crazy in their own world caring about no one and nothing except for themselves and no one else taring down the walls of family and friendship breaking the moral codes that bring people together taring people apart. These people care nothing about what's living always trying to call for the messenger of death to rip what others sow, never caring about who are what they let go. People hate to love, people who would rather push then shove, people who hate for the sake of heating living in others missions, missery loves company so I hope missery doesn't accompany me let me be me so I can fly free, so these people who hate me can quickly let go of me so I can fly freely, so I can get away from these people who care nothing about me, these people who are not apart of me. These people living in the crazy insane world with hate surrounding hoping for the hate to seap in, hoping life eats me alive from the inside, rather then to let me be me and fly free, free from this crazy world that surrounds me so let me be me or is that too much to what's right these people rather have the world swallow me whole then let me be me and happily live my life. Living with hate and hatred with these people who care nothing about me surround by hate don't doubt me. Living in a world where nothing and no one make sence to me living in this world where I can't be me. Surrounded by these people who constantly hate me. Living in crazyness and hate in world that doesn't make sence to me. With no time to hate you, I trying to be me living in this world with nothing but crazyness and hate to surround me. So far from comfort and so far from home living with these people with crazy in a league of its own. These people I never knew. I'm too busy being me I never wanted to be you living my life for me with no love from you I tired of being unhappy tired of receiving hate from you. These people who care nothing about me, these people let the hate seap in and surround me causing me much pain torcher and torment letting the hate seap in, causing me to be unlike me living my life for you not me. While I'm trying to me I never wanted to be you. I'm trying to love myself tried of the hate from you I want to be me I never wanted to be you.

Every day the world rains on me staying focused on the grind in this world with no love for me. Out here walking in the rain trying my best to stay dry with my head up and my eyes focused on the prize in these mean streets were its do or die trying my best to stay dry. Watching the rain fall on me ain't no love out here that's what the cards showed me as the world rains on me. No time to feel sorry for myself wasting time is so bad for my health out here living the life the cards delt trying my best to stay dry you can you can see the pain in my eyes living in this cold world were its do or die watching the world cry on me living in this world, it's so hard to be me watching the world rain on me. Pick my feet up one at a time trying my best to shine without sunshine only if this world was mine. Keeping my head up I'll get mine in due time living in this world of crime, grit and grime, killers and dope dealers, it's all the same, everyone trying to stay dry in this world of pain trying stay dry walking in the rain as the world rains on me, no time to be you I'm too busy trying to be me. Why don't they just let me be me living in this cold world with no love for me, trying to beat the rain walking in this cold world staying or the grind trying to avoid blood stains and pain surrounded by heartache and pain out here in these mean streets trying to stay dry and avoid the rain trying my best to maintain with all this madness on my brain when will it all stop probably when my heart stops, ain't no love in this world of pain, trying to stay focus but it's so hard to maintain, trying to get rid of this madness that clouds my brain trying to maintain and avoid the rain living in this world where you can't afford to feel pain just push the pain to side and stay focused on the time at hand out here trying to stay dry avoiding the rain and quicksand. Too much pride to ask for help too busy trying to hide the pain inside living in this cold world where it's do or die trying to fight the pain while I watch the time fly bye. Keeping head up staying focused on the grind in this cold world of crime I'm getting mine in due time living in this world that ain't mine trying to stay dry and feel the sunshine and the rains fall on me, why won't they just let me be me and roam free because me is the only way I know how to be trying to stay dry when the rain falls upon me. This world is so cruel ain't no love out here, only sadness and heartbreak out here living in this world with no love for me, so many problems in this world why would the focus on me, ain't no sunshine for me, just pain heartache and torment for me living in this cold world with no back against the wall, I'm standing to stand tall when everyone out here waiting for me to fall. Living this life I can't quit, I can't stop I gotta keep it moving it's the only answer for living in this world where it's so hard for me to be me trying to raise to the top but they just won't let me. Out here trying to avoid the rain out here staying focused on the grind trying to avoid the rain out here in these mean streets it trying my best just to maintain with the weight of the world that clouds my brain. I'm just trying to beat the stress and strain out here living in these means streets trying to avoid the rain.

Why won't my heart just let go
Watching the pieces fall apart
cutting me deep ripping through my heart
don't know how it ends remembering
how to start, trying to let go but
my heart says no it feel like my life
is coming to an end why can't I just let
go. Stranded in a lonely world with no
place to go, all alone with nothing but
old memories and a broken heart trying
to start over but I don't know where
to start. Trying to start again so I can
live again and love again hoping to
start over again, so lonely all bye my
self again. Remembering how we use to
love one another, we use to hold one
another. Remembering your smile and the
beautiful face I use to wake up to looking
at our pictures thinking about how much
I love you, but now I'm all alone living
in a house that's not my home feeling the
pain from my heart trying to start over
again but I don't know where to start
How do you start over again after losing
your heart. Feeling like my life is coming to
an end trying to start over but I don't
know where to begin. Why won't my heart let
go, watching the pieces fall apart trying to
start over again but I don't know where
to start. I see your face and I remember
how good life can be. I remember when
you use to love only me. Now those memories
are just memories you act like you don't
even remember me. All alone in a home that's
not my own looking at your pictures thinking
about picking up the phone knowing your
not home, how could this be so much time
together and you act like you don't remember
me and the time we shared, now its nothing
but memories heartache and pain, love is driving
me insane I see your face everywhere I go
alone in a world with no place to go trying
to start over again trying to let go and I see

your face again. Trying to let go so I can begin
again. I have to start over so I can live
again. Why won't my heart let go, watching the
pieces fall apart staring out your pictures, trying
to mend my broken heart, trying to start
over again so I can live again trying to get
over you so I can begin again. Watching the
pieces fall apart trying to get over you and mend
my broken heart

BETTER IN A BOX

Money motivated hustlers raising to the top. Staying focused on the grind until we reach the top, check the plot these haters hate on me non stop, showing no love for these niggas who have no love for me only fake hand shakes and mean mugs for me, these fake motherfuckers get no love from me. Staying fucka free it's the only way to be shaking these haters off so bitch nigga get off me. Never worried about you I'm too busy doing me staying on the grind remaining sucka free fuck these bitch ass niggas, they get no love from me. I keep my ning next to me for these niggas out here testing me. Always loaded and ready to go, staying on the grind collecting my dough, out here doing my thang pushing you know. I'm hot they fucking with a nigga harder then crack rocks I'm too hot for the block and too tuff for the turf out here doing my thing pushing you know moving that work. And still I'm out here with steel face to face with these niggas facing steal staying on the grind owning mine loaded up and ready holding steal with a cold heart and a iron will money motivated money makers on a mission for a mill staying on the grind collecting doller bills and still bitch nigga you'd like better in a box out here fucking with these niggas harder then crack rocks. With my nina next to me for these bitch niggas testing me snitching on your boy getting them boys to handcuff and arrest a G these niggas always testing me ain't no love out here, ain't no running from these niggas bitch nigga I'm standing right and I ain't going no where, just me and my chrome bitch loaded up and ready for gun play, nigga it ain't up to me you better listen to the gun spray. Sitting back loaded up and ready sitting on my black AK where I'm from niggas don't play. No love for these niggas with no love for me tell you to your face face to face fuck you busting freely. Now I'm standing in your face, face to face with the nigga trying to take my place, earse my face hating on your boy trying to take my space I know me not related but I know the hollow tips can relate shaking the fake off only kicking with the real money motavated money makers stacking on a mill ready to kill with looks that kill to me bitch nigga you'd look better kissing steal and still bitch nigga you'd look better in a box filled up by the clip catching all shots to me you'sa bitch weather you like it or not, out here baded up and ready to fill up yo box bitch nigga weather you like it or not, ain't no love for you nigga get ready to catch shot say it to your face bitch nigga you'd look better in a box out here fucking with these nigga, harder then crack rock so bitch nigga get ready to catch shots.

Gorilla warfare ain't fair, win at all cost can't afford a lost in and out unnoticed I can't get caught switching up the game and now the game is bought. Military tactics with a criminal mindset nothing fair in love and war I don't keep score surviving in this world with no time to sleep stay baded up ready with an eye out for those who try to creap military issue is the issue never secondary always first and foremost keep it primary guard your space play to win, do what you got to do to protect your space fuck the whites in their eyes I don't want to see your face win at all cost especially when I gotta invade your space why do they need you when I can take your space, ain't no love out here. Gorilla warfare ain't fair aiming for the face no shooting in the air especially for these motherfuckers who don't play fair ain't enough room out here we can't share fuck the whites in their eyes and fuck shooting in the air Gorilla warfare ain't fair it's time to switch the game up you can press down I'm a military press up no time for luck win a cost mind over muscle to increase the hustle I got to win out here for me and those who died in the struggle I can't afford to lose tried of going through life battered broken and bruise it's time to switch the game on them keeping it mind over muscle with my mind in the hustle I got to win at all cost fuck dying in the struggle. Gorilla warfare ain't fair so I can't play fair I ain't waiting for the whites in their eyes and I ain't shooting in the air fuck close range why come there when I can send one over there keep some heavy metal that you and yo boy can share I can send a bullet to you with a middle finger in the air you can't play fair with these niggas that don't play fair military issue is the issue in Gorilla ware fare I can't lose I can't afford to fight fair I waiting for the whites in their eyes and fuck shooting in the air nothings fair in Gorilla criminal warfare.

DA BLOCK * <u>THE BLOCK</u>

Homie I'm here to let you know I'm trying to do my best out, this shit here is just for show, I'm trying to make it just like the next man hustling staying on the grind just like the next man living this hard life ain't nothing nice making this hard clash, paying the price for life just like the next man I might get shot up and robbed just like the next man. Never trying to be the best but always trying to do the that I can going through the stress and strain of life trying to avoid the quicksand. Some niggas hate and some niggas show love while we watch each others back and give handshakes and hugs and always keeping love for the block caught up in this hard life weather we like it or not, niggas die out here, handcuffed and arrested and shot some die from Aids and others die just from one shot. Living this hard life with pros and con's with hustlas who don't make it far in the game, while everybody trying to make it to the top doing anything just to maintain, why you think me out here taking blunts to the brain keeping an eye out for these haters and the five O to keep from gettin slain. Living this hard life smoking blunts just trying to maintain, some live by the block some kill by the block other rob steal and kill so they can live by the block some set up shop and get shot down setup bye the block some ride by the block, some slang by the block while everyone trying to make it out the game before they got killed by the block, some steal from the block, some deal on the block other sit back while they watch hustlas get shot on the block. We live on the block, we deal on the block remember faces and catch cases so them nigga can't live on the block keeping an extra clip handy wheather they like it or not. Just remember homeboy we where raise on the block. We never know what time has in store for us we make money clock glocks and bust shots, throw away the throw away and then ride the bus. Out here living the hard life broken battered and bruised knowing the ups and down sometimes never knowing which road to choose living in world where we were built to lose. Be careful out there homie and watch your back and keep your strap strapped up in case these niggas over react, time to check in ??? and love, my nigga stay out of the pen, freedom not free that why it's block life for me.

Homie I'll holla back.

TRAPPED

Trapped in the life I live trying to stay above ground protecting my own, living the hard life strapped up gripping chrome living in these streets with no place to call home never knowing when they might cockback and split my dome. All alone on these mean streets, living against the law out here hustling just to make ends meet. Living this hard life competing on these streets living the life I live trapped in an insane state pockets hungery out here trying to fill my plate trying to make my fast cash last longer so I can get back on my get back, before them boys come and take that living this hard life and I can never fake that put my stash in a safe place before them boys come and take that. I'm trapped in the life and I can't afford to second guess, got to get rid of it all so I can releave my stress, living this hard life stuck in a never ending test, with no rest for the wherey where I been up all day making money the hard way, it's them against me. I gotta eat and that's all I'll say. Trapped living this life making money the hard way. It's them against me and that's all I'll say. Living this hard life making money the hard way. Out here on these mean streets hustling just to eat. Doing what I gotta do just to make ends meet.

LIVING AN INSANE STATE

This is my life, stuck between a rock and a hard place in this hard life with only one life to live and I'm rolling the dice and paying the price for living. This life is nothing but a gamble living of these hard streets cold as ice but that's life. Living to eat these streets will leave you frozen stuck in this insane living the life that I've chosen trying to get back on my get back selling sac for sac stuck in this cold streets avoiding the heat stacking up my dollars to make ends meet but that's life when you let go trying to hold on watching time fly out the window. Living this life because it's the only life I know stuck in an insane state trying to let go a life of pushing that snow never knowing who's friend and who's foe. Everybody trying to do me in dodging cases left and right trying to avoid the pen. Fighting a life a can't win watching time fly out the window living in this insane state where they push that snow with no love for the competition and no love for the game. Living in a world where everybody trying to maintain living this life dodging bullets aimed at the brain living a life of snow taking blunts to the brain. Living the only life I know in this cold world where we push that snow. Living a gamble stuck in these mean streets rolling the dice and paying the price stuck, living in this hard life living in a world with no love for me. This may not be the life for you but it's the life that lives with me, never knowing who's friend or foe with no trust for family living a life that's not the life for me stuck in an insane state with mind over muscle living this cold life where it's time over hustle. Stuck between a rock and a hard place where no place to go stuck in the grind where we push that snow, taking blunts to the brain watching the world fly out the window with life around my kneck looking out for these haters who hate me steal from me and lookback and break me call the police on me so they rob me handcuff and take me stuck in this world that wasn't meant for me living a life of hustlas killer. Snitches and drug dealers this ain't the life for me out here taking blunts to the brain pushing OZ's. Living a life that is not meant for me.

PLAYING SMART

Tripping trying to trap me and set me up entrapment. Trying to catch me doing what I'm doing when I'm moving can't stay around with the police pursuing playing smart no for fuck ups, no mess ups sticking to the game plane doing what I do best avoiding the quicksand, dodging these people trying to trap me and set me up for life. I'm trying to eat out here and they're trying to take my life, while I'm dodging every obstacle in my path protecting my life, living this gamble called life keeping the dice rolling, tripping trying to catch <u>me up</u> for the life that I've chosen trying to split my frame, take <u>me</u> <u>out</u> the game and leave your boy frozen. Can't stay in the same spot from too long. Playing the game and playing smart I've been playing for too long, burnt the spot up now it's time to move on. Doing what I do best protecting my mind and my chest, putting the blunt to the flame putting these blunts to rest. Playing in these hard streets and I passed the test, playing the game smart to me hustling is an art and I'm in artist hoping never to cockback and release the beast, playing the game smart grinding on these mean streets, hustling just to eat living with my little piece of pistol protecting my lifestyle, trying to stay out of the pen and eat and eat at the same time, living in insatify trying to keep a grip on mine living in a world headache shine grit and grind playing the game smart getting what's mine living with my mines next to me protecting my mind. I'm trying to eat out here no time to waste time stuck in this game trying not to lose my mind living this gamble called life taking one stop at a time. Trying to make it to the top before they take mine.

FACE TO FACE IN WITH THE STEAL
PART 1

Am I crazy waking up in a cold sweat to the feel of cold steal. Visions still blury wondering if the steal I feel is real, or am I just dreaming high from the night before, feeling the cold steal on my face visions still blury feeling the weight on the bed watching the bed shake. How could somebody creap into my crib and catch me sleeping, high from the night before and the creaper caught me sleeping or am I just dreaming. The feel of cold steal to my face and the creaper scheming hoping it's not real I'm high I'm just dreaming thinking how could I let this motherfucka put his hands on and put the chrome to my dome in my own home trying to use my piece of the pie with my own chrome. Steal still stuck to the dome I can't believe this nigga snuck in my own home. Staring down the barrel now face to face, facing a full clip with a loaded weapon pointed at my face hoping his fingers don't slip caught me sleeping broke into my house to come and take my shit with no witnesses around to hear the bullets spit round for round, staring down the barrel hoping he doesn't bust round. He caught me sleeping I know here niggas get down. Hoping his finger don't slip, thinking about the safe that I keep in a safe place hoping he don't release and earse my face, wondering how he caught me sleeping, and found my safe space hiden out of sight hoping to survive and stay alive through the night. Face to face with the man who creapt into my home. Face to face with the killa face to face with the chrome hoping he don't release and push back my dome wondering how the hell I ain't safe in my own home staring down the barrel of my own chrome. I know the game better then that ready to except mines, ready for him to put my head on flat instead he didn't release he just cockback safety off face to face with the chrome aimed, cocked and ready loaded and aimed at my dome hearing the chamber cockback that metal tone. Caught me sleeping gone with my mind blown face to face with the killa and the chrome in my own home aimed and ready reaching for my dome. Trying to figure out how the killa creapt in my home and caught me slipping blown, gone in the zone I can't believe I'm not safe sleeping in my own home, after a long night with many blunts blown. Face to face with the killa trapped in my own home staring down the barrel of that fully loaded chrome staring face to face trapped with the killa pointing the chrome to my dome. Can't believe he caught me sleeping in my own home. What do you want from me sitback with chrome on me.

NO GRIT JUST GRIM OR JUST GRIME

Out here trying to make it on these mean streets, down and out grimie as I wantta be living in this world with no love for me. Only a dime to may trying to hold on, keeping a grip on my life trying to not to let go, down and out in a world I let go watching time fly right bye me down and out watching the police slide right bye me, no grit just grimie down and out but not for the count the world hating on me but they can't count me out. I'm out here living on these mean streets with nothing to lose so you can't take shit from me, down and out no grit just grime living on these mean street with nothing but time, and nothing to lose so you can't take mine, born and raised by the streets trying to make ends meet the knock my hustle so I can't make ends meet. Life is hard living on these mean streets. Down and out but never count me out trying to stay on toes with a cig in my mouth and I'm out just another day in the life to me no grit just grime on the hunt for money, with only a dime to my name living in these mean streets trying to maintain, living with the stress and strain that I hold in my brain living in these mean streets trying to maintain, down and out. So I'm out here trying to feed my pockets and make it out of these mean streets. Trying of having to hustle just to make ends meet, with a lid on me living with no grit just grim only a dime to my name so come and take mine, trying to get back on my get back so I bounce back and get what's mine trying to stay focus with wasting my time, down and out living with no grit just grime. Living in these mean streets pounding the concrete in the hot sunshine, hoping I ain't wasting my time down and out living a life of just grim, trying to clean up so I can bounce back trying to stay above water, trying just to stay afloat living on these mean streets, trying not to drown, trying to step up, just another day in the trying to climb up, down and out but can't count me out trying to survive out here with a cig in my mouth life is hard out here living on these mean streets only a dime to my name trying to make ends meet out living the hard life pounding the hard concreate with no grit just grim trying to stay focused keeping that money on my mind.

I want a piece of the pie. I know you know why, I see you eating good living the life sky high, counting stack after stack doing that block thing moving pack after pack. So sit back and relax and listen to the demonstration. I want a piece of the pie keeping the chrome cocked I can see the fear in your eyes I could take it all and I know you know why I saw you eating good living sky high. So here's the propersition sit back stay in your place and you won't go missing I checked your spot so don't think about the twelve gauge sleeping in the kitchen chrome cocked and you know I ain't missing, so listen I've seen your face around the block Mr. Dough boy making moves non-stop Mr. Dough boy running in and out the spot thinking no ones watching when your hotter then the block I'm taking a piece of the wheater you like it or not I came with the chrome to come and take your spot too much money making for you to be on top I gotta get a piece wheater you like it or not chrome cocked I'm not leaving until I'm making money non-stop with the chrome to the dome and now I'm on top no quick movements or I'll let that chrome pop, caught you sleeping so now I'm on top with the chrome ready taking over your spot. I'm taking a piece of the pie wheater you like it or not. What makes you think I'll let you take what's mine face to face with a killa trying blow my mind tracing my moves watching me on the grind sitting in my shit trying to take what's mine face to face with a killa with no fear on mine staring down the barrel pointed at mind trying to take mine thinking the safe in the safe place I knew if he found it he would've earsed my face trying to take mine invading my space hoping he won't release and earse my face and take my place. Staying cool calm and collective under intragation in my own home face to face with a kill threating me in my own home face to face with the chrome, hoping he doesn't take my dome. Waiting for the right moment to make my move face to face with the chrome hoping I don't lose thinking how to disarm wondering how he got in without setting off the alarm hoping my safe is still in a safe place hoping I can disarm before he earse my face but his face looks familiar my vision getting cleaner, feels like I'm looking in the mirror face to face with a killa you can feel the tension in the air face to face with a killa and that chrome glare stuck between a rock and hard place waiting for the right moment to take my place face to face with the killa with a familiar face hoping to take chrome before he takes my face.

- Yeah you know me I know you see my face I came for a piece of the pie and keys to the safe I'm the one with the master plan ride with me and we can avoid the quicksand. If it's anyone here that can protect you I can. I know you know on the streets I'm the man the man with the chrome and the master plan. If there anyone that can protect you on these street you know I can. I've been watching you the whole time living the life pushing packs back to back taking what's mine, without me you'll be wasting your time stay focus you will see in due time. We can have it all if you just stay up on the grind out here on these streets you'll just be wasting your time I've been watching you the whole time riding in these street trying to take what's mine. Stay focus and stop looking at the chrome unless you want to lose it all with one kiss from the chrome.

Staring in your face chrome cocked and aimed at your dome staring at the killa, face to face with the chrome looking in the mirror staring at the killa and the chrome face to face chrome cocked loaded and ready protecting my face chrome protecting my safe looking in the mirror down you see that the killa in the mirror with the chrome cocked back is me. Don't you see the killa is me looking in the mirror chrome cocked and ready.

I guess I on my own untill I meet chrome drinking until my glass is gone living this hard like until they send my ass home. Living in hell so take yo punk ass home I ain't going no where I'm out here on my own untill I meet chrome trying to finish my drink before they put one in my dome living in hell with no place to call home I'm a die only unless I can put one in yo chest so go get chrome I ain't going no where you got time stop wasting my time living in hell with no time to shine so come bitch nigga run up and take mine. No time to waste waiting for you to do what you do I ain't going no where I got time to spare so put yo finger to the trigger bitch nigga I let shit fly no love for this world so come and take mine or stop wasting my time living in hell with my time to shine I don't have shit so you can have what's mine. I'm out here on my own until I met chrome trying to finish my drink before you blast with the chrome I ain't going nowhere I ain't running home I ain't running bitch nigga so come and bring that ass on untill I finish my drink my glass not done. I don't give a fuck bitch nigga I done until my caskets done staring in yo face, face to face with the nigga trying to take my life bitch nigga I gives a fuck about you or the afterlife I don't think twice bitch nigga do what you do until then bitch nigga I'm out here waiting on you out here on my own until I meet chrome and catch one to the dome not scared of shit bitch nigga so bring that ass on drinking until my last drop is gone if you don't want none then stop wasting my time I ain't scared of shit I put my life on mine waiting on chrome so come and take mine and stop wasting my time untill then I guess I'm out here on my own drinking my glass waiting for a shot to the dome waiting to go home. If you don't want none then take yo bitch ass home, living in hell waiting for a shot to the dome waiting for you to cock the ??? living in hell nigga so send my ass home. Waiting on you out here on my own waiting on chrome getting my drink on.

I picked this collection of songs and poems to inspire the world with my expression and view of life from my point of view. I started writing these pieces of art many years ago when I was surrounded by hater in a great time of need. I had to take a journey inside myself and create my own happiness and these songs, poems, and information poured out through a pen, helping me in a great time of need. I wanted to share with you the reader this collection of ideas, hoping to entertain and tickle the imagination of the world. The creation of this collection was a great step in the right direction in a great time of need. I am pleased with the outcome of this collection and hope to bring greater understanding peace, love, happiness and entertainment to you the reader in this great journey called life.

Printed in the United States
By Bookmasters